ROADSIDE JUSTICE

AND WHY SOME PEOPLE NEED A
GOOD ASS-KICKING OCCASIONALLY

ROBERT E. LEE ELLIOTT

KANGAROO PUBLISHING

Table of Contents

Introduction

This is one man's opinion based on eighty two years of life's experiences. Hopefully a satisfactory explanation will be explained for the practice of "roadside justice" and why it was born. While serving twenty five years on a large and proud police department I was forced into accepting the concept of roadside justice because too often it was that or no justice at all. It was a procedure where it was absolutely necessary at times to gain a degree of respect from some foul mouth punk and educate him on being respectful to others. No ass kicking was ever administered to someone that didn't need it and it was a proven way to adjust their attitude toward others.

Current events, the media's efforts to undermine President Trump, spineless republican senators, riots, displays of ignorance among college students, the movement by the liberal left to erase our nation's history and numerous other subjects will also be addressed in the book. It's quite obvious to anyone with half a brain that the Democratic Party has only one objective and that's to resist and obstruct everything that President Trump is trying to accomplish. The Russian connection became a dead horse and they continued beating it until it became a national joke. Now they have that skinny little runt with the big mouth Al Pimpton, bitching about his tax money being used to support the Thomas Jefferson Memorial in Washington, D.C. Of course what else would you expect from such a devoted racist? It's been said by people in the know that the best part of Pimpton must have ran down his momma's leg.

The book will give you a new and interesting perspective on America and the idiots that control the country's destiny.

Dedication

This book has been dedicated to all of the police officers that have been assaulted, falsely accused, hospitalized, crippled and died in vain for a politically correct society that couldn't care less.

And to lawyers, judges, illiterates and other mentally handicapped people that have no understanding of truth and justice.

Foreword

In short the United States of America has gone to hell in a hand basket and there are millions of so-called citizens determined to keep her there. Our country is a country of laws which makes it a fruitful playground for lawyers. Lawyers have driven and pulled America so far left with their liberal agendas that it may never recover in our lifetime if ever. Whenever liberals of the democratic persuasion controls large cities such as Detroit, Baltimore and Chicago to name a few the city falls into a state of squalor and corruption.

When Obama became President he appointed the same caliber of people that brought down healthy and solvent cities to decay and destruction. He filled cabinet positions with the same incompetent morons. He was swept into office by a sea of ignorance and stupidity which still exist to this day.

His actions and anti-police attitude against police departments demoralized and destroyed the effectiveness of some proud and hard-working police departments as in the case of New York City. When the empty suit Mayor addressed the department's police officers at an officer's funeral they turned their backs to him as he was speaking which indicates the contempt they have for him.

When police officers are not backed by their administrations and courts then they are forced to apply and obtain some form of justice on the streets known as roadside justice. I have testified in every kind of court criminal and civil for twenty five years just to see criminals and every kind of defendant walk out free far too often. Apparently a defendant's obvious guilt doesn't mean dilly squat to most lawyers and judges. They look at it as a game and they play it well at the expense of society. If anyone ever needed to locate a bonafide asshole for some reason all they need to do is contact the bar of their county or state and they will provide you with thousands of names.

Read this book and you will completely understand how proud ass kicking police departments evolved into ass kissing police departments and why the concept of roadside justice was born out of sheer necessity for the sake of justice. If some of the politicians would have had their ass kicked occasionally they would have become better citizens and less apt to steal and cheat some poor slob client out of their money when they represent them. I personally have never met a lawyer yet when dealing with them that didn't screw hell out of me in one way or the other. The only difference between a lawyer and a street robber is that the lawyer doesn't have to wear a mask. Law school gives them a license to rob someone and it saves them the price of a gun. Most of them can put John Dillinger to shame and what blows my mind is the fact that it's all quite legal. Once they're recognized for their ability by their peers they may be elevated to the position of God father or judge.

This book is written in plain simple language for the common layman to read and understand. I didn't go to the dictionary and use big fancy words to impress anyone. Some readers may even think that I probably didn't finish the sixth grade in elementary school, but one thing I want everyone to know is that I didn't ride into town on the back of a cabbage truck. I'll compare my educational credentials to anyone else. When I went to college I went to learn something, not to just sit on my ass and look for a so-called safe place to shoot my mouth off at our country. I obtained an associate of arts degree from

Miami-Dade Community College, a bachelor of science in criminal justice from Florida International University and a master's degree in public administration from Biscayne College.

I call it the way I see it and if it offends anyone then put the book back on the shelf so someone else can read it. Between the degrees and twenty five years on the police department I find myself better qualified to discuss most subjects better than other people, especially today's college graduates.

The Story

It takes a special kind of person to be a police officer. In my opinion no one should be hired or even considered under the age of twenty five years old. Candidates should be interviewed extensively to determine their level of maturity and ability to accept criticism from all walks of life. During these times a police officer is expected to fill the roles of a minister, doctor and father to mistreated children and dysfunctional families.

When joining the Dade County Sheriff's Office I attended class eighteen which was conducted at Miramar Elementary School in Miami, Florida. Also attending class eighteen as a new police candidate was the future director of the police department. During the academy we were taught about criminal law, civil law, testifying in court, emergency procedures, attending child births, securing crime scenes, use of force, hostage situations, radio procedures and many more topics too many to mention. You name it and it was covered but the one thing they failed to covered was how I could always avoid getting my ass kicked. After a few of those I went back to check the job description of my position to see if getting my ass kicked was in the job description. I decided right there and then if there was going to be anymore ass kicking I'd be doing it. I suppose that kind of attitude was instilled into the minds of most the officers and was the beginning of the concept of roadside justice.

In those days when I first joined the department there wasn't fire rescue units and the patrolman on duty had to handle everything. Then accident units were formed to handle nothing but vehicle accidents which removed another responsibility from the overworked patrolman who was having to investigate vehicle accidents besides everything else. When I finally graduated from the academy and was assigned to the uniform street patrol it was a real learning experience. Most of the things that I was taught in the academy didn't seem to apply on the streets when it came to dealing with people in the real world. I learned quickly that when you go to serve an arrest warrant at someone's house you never stand in front of the door as you knock on it. After six months on the road and being assigned to a low life and rough section of town I became convinced that getting your ass kicked and your uniform shirt torn off was routine and expected behavior from the lowlifes in that particular zone.

I soon realized and accepted the reality that I wasn't hired to be a punching bag for the pleasure of every low life that I came into contact with. Having to literally fight for your life with some punk to effect an arrest and then see some judge turn him lose with nothing more than a slap on the wrist destroys your confidence in the court system. It makes you start to wonder about our system of justice. Who ever said that crime doesn't pay didn't know what the hell they were talking about. I look around and see drug dealers weighted down with huge gold chains around their necks driving brand new expensive automobiles. They sure as hell don't work and spend their time pimping for prostitutes or selling drugs while I'm busting my ass working and trying to pay my bills each month to survive.

Every citizen should be treated with the utmost respect but there are exceptions to the rule. After a few years on the road I adopted a few rules of my own. If you assault me then expect to lose some of your front teeth and have your nose rearranged on your face. Why, because I'm sick and tired of being a punching bag for their entertainment.

For example, one night I was dispatched to a disturbance call at a Howard Johnson's restaurant where some nimble brain punk was giving a waitress a hard time. When I arrived I was advised that the trouble maker had left and gone home. It wasn't thirty minutes later I received a call to go to a nearby residence reference another disturbance. When I arrived there I discovered the same loud mouth punk that had caused the disturbance at the Howard Johnston's restaurant. As I was talking to his mother the punk sucker punched me and the fight was on. As I was beginning to tire, out of nowhere a young female officer appeared and jumped on the punk's back and began to hammer on his head. We finally got the sorry little bastard under control and handcuffed.

If I ever had any thoughts that females shouldn't be police officers, her actions that night rescuing my ass erased any doubts that I might have entertained regarding female police officers. From that night on I became a strong supporter of having female officers. I was just an old timer with a closed mind that didn't know any better, but that little gal opened my mind and made me realize what a jerk I had been. That incident happened over thirty years ago and I'll never forget the sorry punk's name because he was the reason I first started to support the concept of roadside justice, so all you people that got your ass kicked you can blame the king of punks, Frank Tello. That jerk's imagine will be etched into my mind forever. Over the years as a police officer it became increasingly apparent to me that kicking someone's deserving ass would probably be the only justice received regarding his offense. Too often a smart ass defendant appears before some kiss ass judge and walks out of the courtroom laughing.

I always tried to be completely fair and impartial when dealing with the public. I never permitted my own personal feelings to impact my judgment and decisions. After dealing with trash and low lifes for years it's a real challenge to your character. As the old saying goes don't judge another man until you walk in his shoes. I defy any person to be physically abused, falsely accused, slandered, criticized and assaulted from all quarters without it affecting his attitude toward other people. It got me to the point that I developed more compassion for animals then most human beings. Humans exhibit the worse in the chain of life. They kill each other without reason, rob, steal and rape without conscience and make me ashamed of belonging to the human species. For myself I have learned to trust no one because I understand human behavior completely. Yes, maybe I am too critical toward other people, but the forces of life and the actions of other people have forced me into that box. Lying lawyers and brain dead judges with their absurd decisions forced me into accepting the concept of roadside justice. Lying trash lawyers and a couple of apparently feeble minded judges made unjustified rulings that destroyed my life as explained in the book "Kangaroo Justice."

On the road you fight for your life in many cases with someone who smells and looks like a bum. When he appears in court he's well dressed, clean shaven and smells like a rose bud. They usually appear in court wearing a three piece suit looking like and talking like a Baptist preacher. The judge looks at the fine looking gentleman and his pleasant demeanor and simply can't believe that he was disrespectful to the officer in anyway. So the judge in all of his imaginary intelligence will find him not guilty and turn him loose. The next thing the officer knows the asshole has filed a complaint against him for violation of his civil rights and police brutality. You can bet that some money grubbing lawyer is licking his chops just thinking about how much the police departments going to pay his client to drop the case. Thanks to a bone headed judge and the tax payers he can buy himself another new car. The county and city governments are always an easy touch for big settlements. It seems that most lawyers are natural born blood suckers that will do anything for money. Truth and justice, right and wrong doesn't mean jack shit to a lawyer. I personally had to deal with a female lawyer in Florida that would lie to hell and back for money. The perfect clients for her were people ignorant as hell that she can push papers in front of them to sign knowing that they can't even understand what they're signing. She goes by the name of douche bag Mary of the fat, dumb and happy law firm in ft. Lauderdale, Florida. To really know this sorry bitch read the book "Kangaroo Justice"

If you ever have to appear in court just bear in mind that the judge is nothing but another lawyer who will no doubt side with the lawyer that's trying to stick it up your ass. They belong to the same clubs, organizations and drinking establishments. If the judge rules in your favor how does he explain that to the lawyer that's against you when they're having another drink at the club? I have personally been robbed big time by lying lawyers and incompetent judges that didn't know their ass from a hole in the ground. Most of them that I've encountered should have had their sorry ass kicked on the roadside or any place for that matter. It would probably have made them better men then just being a pimple on a real man's ass. The last two judges that I met in a courtroom did nothing but sit on their fat ass half asleep and draw a big undeserved salary. The schooling they receive in some dip shit law school seems to warp their judgment and gives them a superiority complex which makes them think they're smarter than everyone else. Most couldn't hit their ass with a bow fiddle if their life depended on it.

Look at congress where eighty four percent of the people are lawyers. No wonder nothing can get accomplished because each one thinks he or she is the brightest person in town and everyone else is some kind of dumb ass. The only thing that the democrats can do is try and obstruct everything that President Trump tries to do. Their party is in complete disarray and dropping out of the party is the only logical solution. Between Obama and Numerous morons they have destroyed the party beyond repair. It wouldn't surprise me in the least if they get Maxine "Racist" Pottymouth or Al Pimpton to run for President. Actually they would have a better chance if they nominated Mickey

Mouse or Goofy to run. Talk about a flaming loud mouth racist Maxine Pottymouth takes the cake hands down. I believe that Obama has ruined it for another black person to run for President in the near future. Seeing how he did his best to destroy our country I don't think the people will take a chance on another black for a long time since he was such a sorry and pathetic excuse for a President.

Doesn't it make you wonder where Al "no justice no peace" Pimpton has gone? I got so used to seeing him going into the oval office and being an advisor to Obama I just started wondering where the hell he has gone. While Obama was President Pimpton made over one hundred seventy six trips to the oval office to provide advice to Obama. For a skinny little loud mouth racist he really got into the Obama click. It really surprises me that Obama, Maxine Pottymouth, Jesse Fraction and their other racist friends never complained about the White House being called the White House. Surely they can make a racist issue out of that too like they do everything else. If they do they can depend on a lot of the freeloading college students to congregate in front of the White House and protest carrying their Mickey Mouse signs. It seems like college students enjoy a good and rowdy protest because they're too damn ignorant to express themselves in a more fashionable way.

The majority of the protesters seem to be college students that still want everything for nothing. The ones that I've seen interviewed on Watters World struck me as being hopelessly stupid and have no understanding of anything political it always bewilders me to see two hundred police officers in riot gear failing to disperse a crowd of morons destroying private property. Instead of spraying the assholes with good drinking water, spray them with raw sewage from septic tank trucks. When they get hit in the mouth with urine and excrement it will promptly change their attitude and mission. When some jerk gets hit in the mouth with a bundle of excrement he'll get more interested in cleaning his face up and spitting then destroying someone's private property. Of course I suspect that a good number of them might consider it a nice thoughtful treat and enjoy it. Deploying hundreds of police to disperse rioters is a waste of manpower and taxpayers money. Give me ten well armed men with shotguns loaded with buckshot and I'll put down any riot in short order. I would advise the rioters and general public that anyone on the street or outside of their house would be shot on sight beginning at a designated time and there would be no exceptions. There are other ways of crowd control and dispersing rioters, but shooting them is the most immediate and effective way of putting it down.

The city of Miami had a police chief by the name of Walter Headly, who warned the rioters in a big scale riot in Miami that when the looting starts the shooting starts. Later on we had a riot in Opa-Locka and the officers just stood around and watched rioters pushing grocery carts down the street completely filled with loot. The city was run by a mayor that probably thought his people deserved some property and had the police stand down and do nothing. As far as I'm concerned anyone arrested for rioting and destroying property should have their citizenship revoked, all their property confiscated by the state and bill his or her parents for all the welfare including food stamps that they had received for the prior five years. Simply put, any nit wit that gets arrested for rioting and destroying property will automatically lose their citizenship. Most of them probably have their pockets stuffed full with food stamps and/or a cellphone that Obama gave them for free at taxpayer's expense. Obama knew that the more free shit he could give away the more support he would get from all the freeloaders.

The police are confronted everyday with thieves that would easily fit the profile of most congressmen. Some of the biggest thieves and liars that I've ever met wore three piece suits and carried a briefcase. Just because a person dresses nice and speaks well doesn't mean that he or she is an honorable and honest person. I've been robbed by the

7

best of them and wouldn't hesitate to make a donation for a head-stone for any of them. Can anyone really blame a police officer for kicking some foul mouth punk's ass prior to arriving at the jail house? Roadside justice was only administered when it was absolutely necessary to adjust someone's attitude. It usually served the purpose of insuring that some justice was recognized before the individual appeared before some bleeding heart judge that would probably turn him loose again.

After a couple years working on the streets it became apparent to me that I definitely had a communication problem when dealing with the public. I finally decided that the only way I could resolve the problem was to talk to people on their level. I had learned that being polite to some people was taken too often as a sign of weakness on my part and invited trouble. So I set new rules on my communication with other people and the basic rule was if someone was polite and respectful to me, I would be polite and respectful to them. If there level of conduct went into the sewer so would mine. Talking to someone on their level is the only way of understanding each other. I never had any problem tracing some foul mouth punk's family tree. The days of everyone respecting and supporting the police are long gone due to agitators like Al Pimpton, Posie O'Ronald, Pewdonna, Ashley Mudd, Maxine Pottymouth, Rachael Madcow and television shows like "Morning Joe." Now there's a couple really warped assholes for you. I understand that Mika wants Joe to finally marry her because she's tired of giving him the milk for free and it's time for him to start paying for it according to rumors. It's obvious that Joe will take any old port hole in a storm. Some guys just get pussy whipped over time and it beats playing with yourself. Joe probably has a hell of a callous on his right hand and you can rest assured it wasn't from doing manual labor if you get my drift. Everything that I write about relates to real life experiences and are not figments of my imagination. Have you ever known real fear? Well, let me tell you how it feels to possibly losing your life. Our shifts would usually rotate each month when I was on the police department and I was assigned to the midnight shift. We had a prowler that was terrorizing the northeast section and as the shift commander I assigned four officers in civilian dress to work the area on foot and on bicycles. In the early morning hours I heard one of the officers yell for help over his radio and give his location. By the transmission I could tell that the officer was in deep trouble and needed help immediately. I raced to the area and observed him fighting with a black individual on the front lawn of a house. I took an arrival, bailed out of the squad car, jumped over a hedge and joined the fight. As we fell to the ground in an effort to subdue the person I heard my leg snap, but the next thing I heard made me forget all about my leg. The other officer, Terry Palmer, yelled "Elliott, he has my gun" at which time the individual assured both of us that he was going to blow our brains out. After I arrived on the scene and took an arrival the dispatcher was unable to raise me on the radio and dispatched another officer on a three signal to my location. Just as I was beginning to think for sure that I was about to lose my life I looked up and saw Officer Bob Tankersly jumping over the hedge and racing toward Officer Palmer and I. To this day I thank each of them for saving my life and especially the dispatcher that recognized that I was in trouble when I didn't answer my radio.

It was later learned that the subject was a security guard at the one hundred sixty seventh street shopping center in north Miami Beach and held a black belt in karate. Sometimes things do end well because he tried to arrest some young white shoplifter in the shopping mall and the shoplifter shot his black ass deader then hell. Of all things my supervisor told me to escort his funeral because he was a security officer which I promptly refused to do. I explained to my supervisor that there was no way in hell I was going to escort a person's funeral that tried to kill me and if he felt that a charge of insubordination against me was justified then go for it. Actually, when I heard that the sorry bastard had gotten killed it made me extremely happy. My only regret was that I didn't get to do it myself. I had made up my mind that if the person was ever caught that killed his ass I would donate money for his defense and reward him for a job well done.

He was a mean little bastard, but the worse shit kicker that I ever ran across was a guy by the name of Blazejack. This guy was either mentally deranged or just plain stupid. He reminded me of what the movie actor John Wayne, once said. Life is tough and a lot tougher if you're stupid. From the moment he was stopped for a traffic violation he let it be known that he was going to kick some police ass and proceeded to fight. I played Dixie on his thick head with my slapstick and it didn't seem to phase him at all it took myself, a civil defense reserve officer and officer Charley Sirois to get the wild man under control, handcuffed and into my police car. When we arrived at station one and took him out of the car to book him it was necessary to remove the handcuffs and when they were removed the battle started all over again. I had to get a larger prison van to transport the idiot down town because it was obvious that he would kick the small van to pieces before we could arrive at the county jail. I drove the prison van into the sally port to unload the prisoner. Before arriving there I had requested that the jail have at least two jailers meet me in the sally port to help me unload a unruly and combative prisoner. When I opened the back doors of the prison van the prisoner was backed up against the back of the van daring anyone to touch him. The two jailers went into the van and all hell broke loose and within a couple minutes the prisoner was thrown out of the van landing on his thick empty head. He was placed in a holding cell waiting to be booked into the county jail and kept running his foul mouth until he had the jailers go into his cell and shut his mouth for him. That sorry bastard tried everything possible to get me indicted for violating his civil rights and aggravated battery. F.B.I. agents contacted me twice at my district station for interviews and then the state attorney's office had me come down and give depositions to Blazejack's attorneys which I refused to do in the presence of an assistant state attorney who was going to record every statement and word that I was going to say. I informed the assistant state attorney that I was sick and tired of being harassed by Mr. Blazejack and for all I care he now has a free ticket to do anything he desires in my district. I am putting everyone on notice that I will not enforce any law that he wants to violate and as far as I'm concerned he can do no wrong and will not receive any interference from the police. At that I excused myself and left the room. A week later I was informed that the state attorney's office had closed the case and exonerated me of any wrong doing.

One evening as I was the shift commander in the northeast district station I had three officers killed while investigating a stolen car incident at a motel on Collins Avenue. As the officers approached the subject's room one officer was hit in the head with a shotgun blast as he passed the kitchen window killing him instantly. The officers were in a narrow hallway with no place to turn when the subject stepped out of the door and gunned down the second officer as he was trying to run down the narrow hallway with no place to seek shelter. He was shot in the back and killed instantly as in the case of the first officer. The third officer made it out of the hallway and outside of the building, but the subject had followed him and gunned him down before he had a chance to defend himself. He was badly wounded and was taken to the hospital where he later died of his wounds. After shooting the third officer the subject ran across Collins Avenue and hid in a large sea grape growth where he was found later dead of a gunshot wound. Living this incident and seeing the dead bodies of my police brothers made me truly understand what law enforcement was really up against.

When I joined up with the police department I was making $362.00 a month which amounted to a salary of peanuts. I had to work extra jobs just to be able to pay my bills and looking at the bleeding and dead bodies of my comrades and friends made me wonder if it was all worth it. It makes you wonder how and why the hell it's so easy to get killed in America. Thousands upon thousands die each year of overdosing on drugs. Thousands are killed each year in car wrecks. Cancer and other terminal diseases fill up the cemeteries by the thousands and that doesn't even count the ones that kill each other out of hate and etc.. People murder each other for hardly any reason or no reason at all and maybe just for the thrill of it. You can get shot in almost any large city for no other reason then walking to the store for a loaf of bread. Police officers get killed for doing nothing more then sitting in their police car writing a report. If you join the military pray that you aren't stationed in a place like Chicago, Baltimore or Detroit where there's a good chance you may get killed. Try and be stationed in Afghanistan or some place in the middle east where it's a lot safer. For myself I'd much rather be there fighting isis and other terrorist then being subjected to the low lifes in those cities.

America, America, what the hell has happened to that great land of milk and honey? The idea of everyone having a lawyer has destroyed our freedom. Most lawyers seem to naturally breed corruption and has become a way of life for them. They're completely self serving and if you have any doubt about that just look at congress and the way it operates. Almost all of the people in congress are lawyers which explains why nothing can get accomplished. It will never change until we get term limits to prevent politicians from holding office until they become old and senile to the point that they don't even know their own name. No one should be able to hold a seat in congress for thirty and forty years until they're drooling on themselves. I've said it before and I'll say it again, being a lawyer should disqualify a person from holding public office. It's common knowledge that almost any lawyer will never pass up a chance to make money. Look at the O.J. Simpson trial and you'll see a good example of what a lawyer is made of and what he or she worships. All of those lawyers knew that Simpson had murdered two people and that didn't mean jack shit to them. They knew they had the perfect opportunity to make a real bundle of money from Simpson and that's all that mattered. Even police officers under circumstances can be tempted to go astray sometimes because of their low pay scale and being overwhelmed with bills at home. As long as I was on the police department I only witnessed a wrong doing a couple times by the patrolman on the beat and he was immediately corrected and shown the error of his ways. It's easy to find yourself in a tempting situation and find yourself in a struggle between right and wrong and good and bad. When I was a young officer making peanut wages and having to exist from payday to payday it would test your character and honesty to the core. I was raised by parents that had introduced me to a fellow named Jesus and instilled in me the understanding of right and wrong. That belief gave me the strength to resist doing wrong. One incident I responded to a call regarding unknown possibly gun shots in a residential area. When I arrived at the questioned house and went inside I observed two dead men lying on the floor next to the dining room table which had large stacks of money all over the table. It looked like there was so much it'd take me two weeks to count it. There I stood looking at more money then I'd make in a life time. You can only imagine all the thoughts that I was having regarding that mountain of money. It could be the ticket for a good life and end all of my financial problems. The little devil on my shoulder kept telling me to at least take half of it because nobody would ever know and besides it was dirty drug money. As I was having this power struggle between right and wrong I couldn't ignore the little angel on my right shoulder that kept reminding me of what my parents taught me as a young kid regarding right and wrong. Oh yes, it would be like taking candy from a baby but how would I deal with my conscience knowing that it was wrong? I realized that I could never steal anything and my parents and that little angel kept me honest and in line. I knew there was no way on God's earth I could live with myself being dishonest and giving into temptation. During my entire career with the police department I always tried to do the right thing. Even when it came to combative wise ass punks. I never arrested or kicked anyone's ass that didn't deserve and need it. In every zone in each district there were always an element of street thugs and hoodlums that operated and worked the neighborhoods.

One night when I was still a young and relatively new on the force my supervisor had me ride the plain unmarked prowl car which was designated call numbers 642. The basic function of the prowl car was to catch prowlers and to my amazement the first prowler I observed was my supervisor. In the early morning hour I parked at the end of the street partially hid with my lights off because we had numerous reports of a prowler in that area and it wasn't long before I observed a uniform squad car come into the area with its lights off and park across the street from a house that had previously reported having a prowler. I observed a figure get out of the car and go between two houses. After awhile the figure went back to his car and drove off with his lights on. I followed the car and noted the car number to make sure I wasn't imagining things. He was a good man and a good supervisor who on that evening obviously made a bad choice in assigning me to ride the prowl car.

Looking back on my days as a police officer it makes me realize that it never ends. People will continue to rob, steal and kill each other until the end of time. The police can control a lot of the crime and suppress it to a degree, but it will never be wiped out. Does crime pay? Apparently it does and very well too. Just look at the state of our nation and who runs it. The people are nothing but pawns controlled by the Washington bureaucrats. It's been that way ever since Moby Dick was a sardine and it will most likely stay that way. President Trump is trying to drain the swamp, but considering how long the swamp has existed and by whom, it is proving to be an impossible job. The swamp is nothing but a stagnant pool of corruption that has been entrenched in Washington for decades and the money changers won't give it up easily. Money breeds corruption and the politicians will do everything in their power not to lose their seat on the gravy train. Everyone in congress should be put on a part time basis for employment because all they do is sit on their ass and do nothing worthwhile. It makes no sense at all to pay them for full time employment.

If I haven't learned anything else in my life, I've learned that there's a time to be happy and a time to be sad. A time to laugh and a time to cry and most of all a time to live and a time to die. Many times during my career with the police department I thought for sure it was my time to die. I know that it's hard for the average citizen to accept and understand why roadside justice ever became necessary and accepted on a special occasion sometime. Only a police officer that has been kicked around, abused and falsely accused for years will understand why and how it came about. A new police officer in a few years on the road will realize that fear and respect go hand in hand. At times a police officer will only receive that amount of respect that fear dictates. The only reason that most citizens show any respect is because they fear the legal power that the officer has over them and can do in a particular situation. Of course there are a lot OF dumb ass citizens that don't have the intelligence to grasp that thought. Most of the people I arrested when I was working traffic talked their way into jail. Over the years I became an expert on human behavior. If I was around or talked to someone for five minutes I could tell if that person was a liar or just a real dumb ass with no upbringing. Being a thief is bad enough but being a liar is the worse trait of all. The worse liar that I ever knew in my life is a female lawyer that I identify as douche bag Mary in the book "Kangaroo Justice." She still practices law if that's what you want to call it, in Ft. Lauderdale, Florida. When she dies I hope they bury her face up with her mouth open so I can take a dump on her grave. She gives a new definition to what a lying psychopath really is and how they lack a conscience and have a personality disorder that they can't control. That sorry bitch thinks nothing of swearing a lie before a court and doing anything to steal someone else's money. It was rumored that she was banging her mentally ill client who was the poster child for trailer trash while her husband just stood around in a dumb mode with his head up his ass. My advice to other people is avoid getting involved with a miserable bitch lawyer like her especially if she's going through menopause. Rest assured, she's certainly no beauty queen and apparently doesn't do anything for her husband sex wise. I suspect that Mrs. Palm and her five daughters takes care of her husband. It would really cheer me up if I heard that the lying bitch had been run over by a bus because I know that sorry bitch would go straight to hell.

The Hillary supporters and Democratic Party democrats are doing every dumb ass thing in the world to stop President Trump. They kept beating the dead horse about Russia until most people have gotten to the point that they don't want to hear about it again. Then they went on the kick about the Confederate statues and men of the south. Now they even protest about a white horse that walks out onto a football field during a football game. Then they come up with the bullshit of white supremacy to bitch about. The assholes even vandal- ized the Lincoln Memorial and that skinny little loud mouth twerp Al Pimpton, even states that he doesn't like the government maintaining the Jefferson Memorial Monument with his tax money. That's a joke, that little loud mouth owes the government a million dollars that he never paid in taxes. That's not enough, now we have some jerk ass movement that's nothing but street thugs wearing mask and protesting any gathering with clubs and other weapons. They call themselves "antifa" which probably spells shit in Latin. When I see them see them they remind me of nothing but mobile piles of feces. They must be an arm of the Democratic Party in their determination to obstruct the Republican Party in their effort to get something accomplished. Looking at the Democratic Party and seeing the kind of politicians they have produced I can't understand why anyone would claim to be a democrat.

It seems like every encounter I've had with lawyers they only prove to me that most of them have no moral code and are blood suckers that won't hesitate to screw everyone and anyone out of money in any- way they possibly can. Let's forget the last sorry bitch that 1 referred to as douche bag Mary and go to another one that I'll never forget. My first wife decided to divorce me after fifteen years of marriage because according to her I made her skin crawl. I was served divorce papers and went to a lawyer by the name of Art Wilner, because I didn't have any idea what I was suppose to do. I went to his office and it was a real learning experience to say the least. He was suppose to be friends with my older brother which didn't amount to much. I gave him the divorce papers and after looking it over he said we'll contest this, this, this and this. I told him that since I made my wife's skin crawl and she wanted a divorce so bad I didn't want to contest anything, just give her a divorce. At that he handed the papers back to me and told me that I didn't need a lawyer. As I got up and started to leave he called me back and told me that it would be best if I was represented by a lawyer and he would do it for me. He could tell that I knew absolutely nothing about getting a divorce and charged me six hundred dollars for nothing but signing the court papers. At that time six hundred dollars was a lot of money to someone that took only twenty five cents to work each day in his pocket in case someone charged him for a cup of coffee. These are only two reasons among many more why I have such intense feelings toward lawyers.

When working the road an officer has to assume that everyone he stops might be a bonafide shit kicker until proven otherwise. It's easy to exhibit high and honorable principles until some punk surprises you by punching your lights out over nothing. Then all of your well intended good principles go out the window. That's just a typical example when and why roadside justice is warranted and applied. It's the only effective way of adjusting some punk's attitude. It's not very difficult to understand why roadside justice came about. Having your ass constantly being kicked trying to do your job and it doesn't take long before you start thinking that people must think that your ass is a football. Liberal politicians, city mayors and county managers have all decided that "political correctness" was the way to go and it became quite acceptable and expected for officers to kiss everyone's ass in order to make them happy. The politicians were more concerned in making their constituents happy so they'd vote for them again then what the hell was right and wrong. The most important thing to a politician is to keep getting voted back into office. Political correctness was applied in all quarters until it destroyed the innovating spirit of the people. Politicians are by the large part lawyers and it's just another reason I have such intense negative feelings toward them. They love political office because they can sit on their lazy ass and draw big salaries for doing nothing.

When working on the road the officer has to assume that everyone he stops might be a bonafide shit kicker until proven otherwise. One thing that all citizens should know is the fact that you will get only that amount of justice that you can afford to buy. Look at the case of O.J. Simpson, who was guilty as hell of murdering two people. With his money he got enough defense lawyers to last him for the rest of his miserable life. The lawyers saw the opportunity to pick his pockets clean just like they'd do to any other citizen. All the lawyers that represented him knew that he was guilty as hell, but their only concerns were getting his money and getting him off the hook for murdering two people. The Goldman lad probably thought it was going to be his lucky night returning Nicole's glasses that she left at the restaurant. When he entered the front door gate to Nicole's place he walked upon O.J. in the process of trying to cut Nicole's head off. Goldman upon seeing what was happening yelled hey, hey, hey which was overheard by a neighbor. At that Simpson attacked Goldman and stabbed him to death. Simpson realized that he had to kill Goldman too so there wouldn't be any witness to what he had done. The physical evidence against Simpson was overwhelming but the defense lawyers set out to discredit everything including detective Mark Furman, when F. Lee Bailey asked him on the witness stand if he had ever used the word nigger. As experienced as Detective Furman was he forgot a cardinal rule when testifying. If a lawyer ask you a question on the witness stand, he is only asking you because he already knows the answer. When the detective responded with a no answer, then Bailey called the next witness to the stand which was a female writer who interviewed Detective Furman months earlier regarding a book she was writing. That sunk the detectives credibility even though the use of the word nigger regarding a book had nothing to do with the guilt or innocence of Simpson.

Why the prosecutor Marci Clark, agreed to let Simpson try on his glove in open court was the dumbest thing I've ever seen. Simpson, wearing latex rubber gloves made a grandstand and feeble effort to get his hand into the glove. Marci Clark, should have known that it would almost be impossible to get his hand into the glove wearing a latex rubber glove on his hand. It was a damaging effect on the prosecution and right away you had the defense lawyer Cochran jumping with glee and running around the courtroom stating over and over "if it doesn't fit you must acquit." as soon as I saw the makeup of the jury I knew that there was no way in hell they would find Simpson guilty. It was obvious that the jury was stacked against the state prosecution and they would be fighting a losing battle for justice. The "if it doesn't fit you must acquit" bullshit played on the ignorance of the jurors. Needless to say the judge appeared to spend most of his time trying to figure out what the hell was going on. To me and by his appearance my first thought was that some relative of his must have taken part in the bombing of Pearl Harbor. I could almost see him sitting in the cockpit of a Japanese zero fighter plane. He sure missed his calling because he certainly looked the part.

Please bear in mind that just because a jury finds a defendant not guilty doesn't mean that he didn't commit the crime.

It simply means that the state wasn't able to prove it. In Simpson's case he could have been caught with Nicole's head in his suitcase and they still wouldn't have found him guilty. Everyone knows including his team of lawyers that he murdered the hell out of Nicole and Goldman and should have been executed instead of running ass all over the country enjoying himself. For his entire life he always preferred white women over his own race and only associated with white people. When he's released from the Nevada state prison where he was serving time for robbery, he won't be able to change his ways and will become another crime wave of his own making. When he was found not guilty of the murder charges everyone in the black communities celebrated and jumped for joy. The way they were celebrating and showing signs of victory anyone would think that they didn't give a damn that two innocent people were murdered. The only thing that mattered to them was that he was a black man that beat a murder rap. They exhibited such ignorance it was unbelievable and knowing that the murdering bastard killed two people didn't mean shit to them. It wouldn't have mattered if he had killed ten people. The only thing that mattered was that he was one of them. It's like attorney Dershowitz, recently said on television, "we didn't win the case, the prosecutor's office lost it." it's like I've always said, lawyers don't give a rat's ass if a person committed the crime. They will do anything and everything to get the defendant found not guilty. When a defendant is found not guilty, lawyers say that it was a fair trial, but when he's found guilty, they always scream that he didn't have a fair trial and start flooding the courts with appeals.

I personally feel that Simpson was set up in Las Vegas, Nevada because the authorities there recognized the fact that he was stupid and it would be an easy task to have him do something stupid. It would be an easy way to have the murdering bastard pay for getting away with murdering Nicole and Goldman. All they had to do was put out the word that someone staying in the motel had all of his memorabilia and the moron would most likely go and try to get it back. Like the stupid moron that he is, he took other dumb asses with him to the person's room and demanded his memorabilia back as one of his dumb ass accomplices pulls a gun and tells everyone to get up against the wall the trick had been done, now the stupid murdering bastard is guilty of armed robbery. When the dumb ass got some of his thug friends to go with him to the room to get his stuff, he proved to the authorities that he was as stupid as they thought he was. It didn't get him back his so-called memorabilia, but it got him nine years in the Nevada state prison for being stupid.

Stupidity seems to flourish in America especially on a college campus. Most college students are easily led in their thinking and seem to join in on group thinking instead of thinking for themselves. They join terrorist organizations like "antifa" and assaults peaceful gatherings and have become completely anti American in every respect. My advice to the people being assaulted is if someone attacks you with a club or some other dangerous weapons, shoot the bastard. If someone attacks you and you kill the sorry son of a bitch it's called self defense.

President Trump tries to instill some patriotism in the citizens by stating "hire American and buy American" and it goes in one ear and out the other one with the average citizen. If you have any doubts about that statement just look about yourself when you're driving on the roadway. It appears that eight out of ten vehicles on the road are foreign made. Every time someone buys a foreign made vehicle they're doing nothing but putting another nail in the coffin of the American automobile industry and putting other citizens out of work. The owners of Toyota, Kia, Nissan, BMW, Subaru and the such couldn't care less about destroying Ford, Chrysler and General Motors. Buying American doesn't mean shit to the owners of foreign vehicles and other foreign products. It reminds me of the same attitude that lawyers and judges have when it comes to justice.

Every lawyer that I've come across would be better suited as a used car salesman because both are trained to screw you out of every dollar that they can get out of you. Lawyers charge a fee of three hundred dollars an hour for their services which seems to be two hundred ninety dollars too much at times. One time I stopped by a lawyer's office to have him look at a short letter that I had received. There wasn't anyone in his office and all he was doing was sitting on his ass looking at a magazine. He looked at my letter for approximately two minutes, told me to ignore

The letter and charged me seventy five dollars for looking at it. If you think that was bad it wasn't a drop in the bucket compared to the one hundred twenty five thousand dollars that the last lawyer and judge robbed me of based on lies which is fully explained in the book "Kangaroo Justice" written by yours truly. My advice to anyone dealing with a lawyer is just "be aware." just because they're well dressed doesn't mean that they won't rob the hell out of you because they have a license to steal and it's perfectly legal. Their entire livelihood depends on screwing people out of money anyway they can and they do it well.

Among all the people I ever arrested the one I enjoyed most was a lawyer trying to bribe me to throw a case in court. I was wearing a wire and met the sleaze ball in a parking lot across from the police station and next to the county jail. When he handed me the one hundred fifty dollar bribe he asked me if I was going to put the arm on him. I told him that I hope he brought his toothbrush with him because his next stop was going to be the county jail. He was found guilty of bribery and sentenced to five years in Raiford prison. Apparently the word got out and I was never offered another bribe. One thing you can bank on is that lawyers can lie to hell and back in court or on sworn affidavits and nothing can or will be done to them. Just remember, anything you discuss with a lawyer he will broadcast it to all of his lawyer friends like the voice of America. Privileged communication between a lawyer and his client is a myth and the code of silence doesn't exist.

Human beings breed like flies and I don't see how the earth will ever be able to survive. There's only so much land on earth and eventually all of it will be lived on and destroyed by the human population.

Some of the eating habits of other cultures makes me sick just thinking about it. I know that most Orientals eat dogs and it's been a custom for generations. I've been eating at the same Chinese restaurant for years but after learning how Orientals raise dogs just to kill and eat, their bar-b-qued ribs didn't appeal to me anymore so I decided to change restaurants. Their bar-b-qued ribs seem to be too small for me and I could just envision that Fido or a cat was lying on the steam table waiting to be eaten. Recently I heard that the south Koreans also raise dogs to eat and it makes me wonder if they're feeding dog meat to the twenty five thousand troops we have stationed there. I've heard of people eating pussies but I've never been able to verify it. There's no doubt in my mind if someone will eat a dog they'll probably eat a pussy too. I have a good friend that I've known for years and when I told him that some people will eat a pussy, he looked at me with a strange look and replied "What's wrong with that a lot of people do?" I couldn't believe my ears and decided right then that I wasn't going to associate with him anymore because he may be tempted to catch my beloved pussy and eat it. I know one thing if a person will eat dogs and pussies they'll eat anything. I told my wife to keep our pussy inside the house because our next door neighbor brags about eating a pussy and I was afraid he would eat our pussy if he had the chance. I was floored when my wife suddenly blurted out that every man she ever dated was a pussy eater. That did it, next week I'm booking a space on the Doctor Phil television show to try and understand why eating pussies is so widely acceptable and why nothing seems to be wrong with it. I can understand why so many people will eat a cock because almost everyone loves chicken. It's common knowledge that KFC stands for Kentucky fried cock.

Sometimes when I start thinking about my situation I remember a song that singer Eddie Arnold use to sing. "Take the world off my shoulders and this time Lord you have given me a mountain that I may never be able to climb." I'm certainly not a rich man and I would best be described as an old sick and crippled man that had his life destroyed by a lying lawyer and two judges that would best be described as morons. If you want to see how easy it is for the court system to rob you, read "Kangaroo Justice." the system stripped me of everything and destroyed my life. The only thing I could do about it was to write a book letting everyone know how easily lawyers and judges can completely destroy your life with lies and the so- called legal system.

I'm a man of no means and knowing that I'm in the twilight years of my life I bought myself a grave site, funeral and headstone so I wouldn't end up in a dumpster someplace. Sometimes just for the hell of it I decorate my own grave site. I've always been taught that things will always work out good for those that believe in and serve the Lord. I sure hope so because that's the only hope I have left. If I had the money I'd appeal my case where the lawyers and courts robbed me of a small fortune that I'll never be able to pay off in my lifetime. I know that someday I will truly have peace in my valley if the Lord will only forgive me for my short comings. It was always a desire of mine to own a nice car, but even that has become an impossible dream since I was robbed. Don't get me wrong because I'm still thankful that I have a twenty one year old truck with three hundred thousand miles to drive. It breaks down a lot because like me it's just worn out. I know that someday I'll get to ride in a nice new vehicle even if it's in the back of a funeral hearse on the way to the cemetery. Sometimes it is hard remaining positive on life when everything seems to be going against you. No one can agree on anything.

If you want to see a good example of chaos look toward our congress. It's like senator John McCain said in his speech before the senate. It's all about winning and what's good for the country isn't even considered. After his speech of unity he turns right around and votes no killing any effort by the Republican Party to straighten up the Obamacare disaster leaving millions of people without insurance. For myself before Obamacare my insurance premiums with blue cross was one hundred eighty nine dollars a month. After Obamacare kicked in my insurance premiums went up to four hundred fifty six dollars a month which I couldn't pay and had to drop the insurance. Almost all of the people in congress are lawyers which explains why congress is so screwed up. Like I've said before being a lawyer should disqualify a person from holding public office. For the most part I've witnessed more justice on the side of a roadway then I've ever witnessed in a courtroom. One criminal case that I attended in Judge Turner's courtroom is one that has been etched into my mind for fifty years. A black defendant was on the witness stand describing what happened to him during an interview with a robbery detective. He testified that he was hit over the head and on the side of his head numerous times with a telephone book in an effort to get an admission of guilt out of him. At that Judge Turner asked him if he sees the detective in the courtroom and identify him for the court. The defendant replied that he couldn't because someone had placed a sheet over his head before he started getting hit with the telephone book.

That was an effective way of interrogation but unfortunately it wasn't an accepted practice and the police had to go back to the old method of ass kissing. The ass kissing method of law enforcement began in the early seventies and was supported by new county managers, city mayors and even high ranking police supervisors. The high ranking supervisors went along with it because they were ball less wonders that were afraid of losing their positions. One perfect example would be Captain Whitey Clifton of the Dade County Sheriff's Office. He was from the old school but due to personal ambitions he turned out to be the poster child of ass kissing. He was in charge of station one which was located in a parking lot in north Dade County. Also located in that parking lot was a shit kicking bar which was overrun by shit kickers every Saturday night. On Saturday night it always seem to attract every drunk in town and having fights and jumping on tops of cars became routine with them. I was assigned to the district station on the midnight shift and almost every night I had to break up fights and arrest someone for vandalizing a car, assault or reckless display of a firearm. It happened that most of the people going to that particular bar and raising hell were black. After one Saturday night of arresting drunks I was called at home on Sunday morning and told to report to the captain's office immediately. When I arrived there I was confronted by Captain Clifton and three black individuals in the captain's office. The captain wanted me to explain why I had arrested three black people that Saturday night. I felt that it was highly irregular for me to have to explain my actions to anyone other then the state attorney's office. I expressed my objection to Captain Clifton on why I should have to explain myself to someone that had nothing to do with law enforcement, but since he was my supervisor I would do it this one time. After saying that I'll never forget Captain Clifton's attitude and what he said which gained the approval of the three blacks that he had invited into his office. He stood up, leaned across his desk in a threatening manner and told me that he was my boss and not to ever forget it. He ordered me to stop arresting blacks in the parking lot of the district station which made his guest extremely happy. Ass kissing was Captain Clifton's specialty and it was just one incident after the other. You would think that he was running for public office and was trying to get every black vote in the county at police officers expense.

Then we have another case of his program of ass kissing when black students took over Florida Memorial College which was rather close to the district station. Florida memorial college was a black college and the students displayed a racist agenda that the college president didn't agree with so the students took over the college and barricaded themselves inside the building. Unfortunately this problem fell under the jurisdiction of Captain Clifton and the first thing he did was call numerous black friends of his into his office and ask them what he should do about it. They sat in his office for hours drinking coffee and trying to figure out what should be done about the situation while the mob at the college kept getting bigger and out of control it was obvious that the captain wasn't able or knew how to make a decision on his own and was depending on people to help him that couldn't find their ass with both hands and a map. With the proper supervision the entire incident could have been put down within thirty minutes, but the captain was too busy kissing some more ass. It made me realize that he didn't have the ability to lead a Boy Scout troop much less a district of police officers. Some on scene supervisor made the decision to do something and the problem was resolved in short order while the ass kissing was still taking place at the district station.

Like I said it was just one thing after the other. This next example affected me personally and occurred at Norland High School which was also located in the north district under the control of Captain Clifton again. At the time I was assigned to the general investigations unit and was investigating a series of burglaries and leads led me to a student that attended Norland High School. As I was walking down a hallway I observed two students fighting in a classroom as a terrified female teacher watched. I went into the classroom, identified myself and broke up the fight. I took the students to the office and informed the black principal what had occurred and left the school building enroute back to my office at station one to do paperwork. To my amazement by the time I arrived back at the station the school principal was already in Captain Clifton's office making a complaint against me. Captain Clifton called me into his office and started questioning me in front of the principal as though I had committed some outrageous crime. The principal was complaining that my presence in the school building made it appear to the students that police officers were lurking about the school waiting to arrest a student. Captain Clifton agreed with everything the principal was saying and started chewing my ass out for being there. Again the captain's reasoning and attitude re-enforced my strong belief that he should have retired years before because he had obviously lost touch with reality. He never supported any police officer that I know of and spent most of his time kissing every complainant's ass. He apparently had a drinking problem too because when he attended one PBA dance he was observed by everyone trying to beat some woman's ass in a telephone booth. Good ole Whitey, a real fine example that other people should avoid.

I'm beginning to think that being screwed up is a natural trait for human beings. Look at the Republican Party, when you think that at last something good will be done for our country those idiots can't agree on anything and they belong to the same party. Just recently three more republicans killed any effort to get anything done regarding the disaster known as Obamacare. Senator John McCain of Arizona, Senator Makowski of Alaska and Senator Collins of Maine all voted against doing anything to provide relief for every American citizen regarding affordable health care. The two ladies must be going through menopause, but Senator McCain really disappointed me for not joining the other loyal republicans in their effort to do something. I truly regret that he has come down with brain cancer, but something has certainly effected his way of thinking and he never misses an opportunity to bash President Trump and stab him in the back.

I don't know about everyone else but I'm getting tired as hell seeing our country being dismantled and destroyed. There are forces in our country that's making every possible effort to destroy our Christian religion and remove any mention of God from our vocabulary. It got so bad that even department stores that use to display merry Christmas signs stopped doing it and would only display signs saying happy holidays. As for me they can stick their happy holiday signs up their ass. I still say merry Christmas even if it does piss off the ACLU and atheist. With all of the asshole lawyers and judges in our country it surprises me that they haven't changed our national motto "in God we trust." Christians founded our country and the laws are based on the ten commandments whether the minorities and atheist like it or not. My advice to all the people that don't like it is simple, move the hell out of America and go back to where the hell you came from. I support the idea of love it or leave it. Either love the American people, our way of life and our laws or climb back over the fence that you first climbed to get into our country. The fence climbers and train riders know that as soon as they can get into America they can immediately apply for all forms of welfare benefits which beats hell out of working in Mexico or some other south American country for peanuts. I've been going to a nice Chinese restaurant for years, but it's being over-run by Mexicans to the point of ruining the restaurant's business. It seems like every Mexican woman I see has two or three kids follow-ing her and being knocked up again. If you're a condom salesman in Mexico then you must be starving for business. Their kids must think they're balloons to blow up and the men probably have no idea what they are. Getting laid must be their national pastime.

When I first became a police officer it was understood by all of us that our responsibility was to cover each others back. In todays kiss ass police departments that creed no longer exist. The first one that will hand you up and stab you in the back is another police officer. I contribute that change to the department being flooded with new immature personnel that should never have been hired in the first place. Nothing was ever permanent on the department. One day you might be on the gravy train and the next day you may find yourself on a major shit detail. One day I happened to tell someone that the cap-tain's executive officer was a prick and unknowing to me the person I made the statement to had his nose stuck in the captain's ass so far it would break if the captain made a quick turn. He couldn't wait to run and tell the captain what I said about his executive officer which led to me being transferred to a shit detail I guess it was my fault be-cause when I noticed that the little bastard had a brown nose I should have realized he was kissing someone's ass. I was transferred to the shift commander's office in the headquarters building downtown. I sat on my ass for eighteen months doing nothing but answering the telephone and never leaving the building for any reason. Sometimes I would venture down to the first floor to buy a soda when I was over-come with boredom. I had been on the department for over twenty years serving in almost every capacity in the department except the robbery section but that's another story in itself. One evening out of the blue my supervisor called me into his office and told me that he was writing me up for always leaving the building, using a county car for extended periods of time and for also demoralizing the unit. I could have fallen out of my chair in disbelief and especially when I discovered who the lying little prick was that was telling the captain all the lies. Let me remind you, I never left the building or even touched a county vehicle in eighteen months and how this lying little prick could tell such bare face lies is beyond me. I sat there for eighteen months watching the lying little prick meeting a young female officer that I knew and leaving with her for hours. Yes, I may add in a county vehicle. No doubt the main thing the lying little prick was interested in was finding a motel room that he could use. I would like to divulge the young officer's name but I won't because it would only cause her problems and at least she didn't lie about me. The captain had the honor of being the only supervisor in my entire career to ever write me up and the sad part is that it was based on nothing but lies. I haven't used any of their names as much as I wanted to because I now consider the captain as my friend and he knows the officers that I've referred to because the lying little prick worked for him in homicide. No doubt by now he realizes that he was hoodwinked by an ass kisser. It's a shame that the lying little prick's wife never caught him cheating on her. As much as I'd like to broadcast his name I won't because it would only hurt his wife. For him I hope he rots in hell which he deserves and when he's buried hopefully they will bury him face up with his mouth open so I'll have a place to take a deserved dump. All of the parties that I've mentioned knows exactly who they are.

I could go on and own about how corruption took over the Dade County Sheriff's Office over time and how it became so easy to get rid of any trouble makers on and off the department. If you were considered a problem to them and jeopardized their operation in anyway you'd find yourself being stopped by special enforcements and arrested for all the stolen property in the trunk of your car that you didn't know anything about. See how easy it was done because it wasn't anything to plant stolen property in the trunk of your car to get rid of you. When I was in the traffic section riding motors I witnessed upper management charging another motorman who was a friend of mine, Lynn Erickson, with the theft of a quart of oil valued at nineteen cents that he had put into the crankcase of his county motorcycle. They charged him with larceny, took him to court and made sure that he was convicted. It made me wonder why the major's wife was never arrested for wearing an expensive stolen bracelet at a sporting event for everyone to see. After that was brought to light the major and his wife left under the cover of darkness, moved to Georgia and lived happily ever after. At one time I tried to transfer to the robbery section and started receiving anonymous phone calls at home advising me to drop my request for transfer to the robbery section because I wouldn't fit in with the operation. Next I made an appointment to be interviewed for a position in criminal intelligence and started receiving more anonymous phone calls at home telling me that I was wasting my time going to an interview because the position had already been promised to a good looking female officer. When I arrived for the interview I asked the captain that was going to interview me if I was wasting my time like I had been told and the position had already been promised to officer Glenis Gregg? The captain looked at me and lied through his teeth when he stated that the position wasn't promised to anyone. Two weeks later the position was filled and you guessed it with Glenis Gregg. It didn't bother the captain in the least to sit there on his fat ass and lie like hell I had a division chief tell me that every time a position came open in upper management he would always throw my name into the hat, but was always over ruled by the other chiefs stating that I was too opinionated. I guess they all got that opinion when I attended a staff meeting and asked why a certain police chief always carried his golf clubs in the trunk of his police car? I only ask that question because that particular police chief wrote up a young police, officer for playing a video game on his lunch break at a pizza hut. To me an officer playing a video game sure as hell didn't compare with a police chief playing eighteen holes of golf on duty. Looking back I can certainly understand why I wouldn't fit in. After years of dealing with upper management I came to the conclusion that some people in upper management should have had their ass kicked before coming on the department. Maybe it would have taught them the difference between right and wrong. Power seems to corrupt people as in the case of the police chief carrying his golf clubs in the trunk of his police car and playing eighteen holes of golf on county time.

The one thing that I hate worse then a thief is a liar and the police department that I served in was loaded with liars. We had one little sawed off Italian police chief that thought he was the reincarnation of napoleon. I believe the department must have found him in New York City because he didn't understand human behavior at all. He had a smart ass arrogant attitude and would do anything to put other people down. Why the hell the department ever hired that little jerk was beyond me. He was always trying to throw his dumb ass weight around in an effort to intimidate subordinates in front of other officers. He got to be a real pain in the ass and that's when I took it on myself to tape Mickey Mouse ears on his picture to give everyone a laugh. Everyday at roll call and anytime someone would walk into the squad room and see his picture they'd start laughing at the little jerk. Everyone would always spend the first five minutes at roll call laughing at the division chief and his Mickey Mouse ears. It was funny as hell the way he had the crime scene section take his picture down and process it for finger prints as I stood there laughing my ass off. Just to make sure that 1 would be in the clear I suppose I destroyed the scene because I made a point of me taking down the organizational chart picture and handing it to the crime scene personnel to be dusted for prints. Like in the case of the Mickey Mouse ears, one night while on the midnight shift I found an old discarded microphone and placed it in a flower arrangement on the captain's desk. There was still a length of wire about twenty feet long attached to the microphone and I ran the wire underneath his desk, up the wall and behind the ceiling tiles. I knew he'd find the microphone when the plant was watered and could hardly wait for his reaction. He always called me into his office on the pretense of talking about some police business when he actually wanted to pump me for information regarding my attitude toward the Director Bobby Jones. As soon as I would leave his office he would call the director and fill him in on everything I said about him. I always considered him as my personal and direct pipeline to the director. He always suspected me as being the one responsible for putting the microphone in his flower arrangement but just didn't have any proof. I always tried to inject some humor into the boring job of being the shift commander on the midnight shift. Often I would spend hours sitting at my desk doing evaluation reports and boredom would take over causing me to entertain myself in some way. One night I drew a picture on my desk of the captain blowing his nose which wasn't very complimentary. At the end of the shift I forgot all about the drawing and went home. When I got home it dawned on me that I never erased the picture off my desk and I immediately called the oncoming lieutenant at the station and told him to erase the picture before Captain Senk saw it. He told me that it was too late because the captain had already seen it and wasn't very happy at all the captain recreated the drawing on a piece of paper, stuck it on the district station's bulletin board stating that anyone drawing such a picture had an elementary school level of maturity. Well, regardless of how he felt it brought a lot of laughs at the station which had always been in short supply before. It was apparent that a lot of upper management people didn't appreciate well intended humor.

With me an officer's personal taste in his sexual appetite wasn't that important as long as they performed their job. In every corner of society we have thousands of good competent men that prefer a pole over a hole and women that couldn't care less about a pole and police departments are no exception. For myself I've always thought of myself as a French carpenter when it came to sex and was always known as a tongue in groove man. Look at the television personalities and you will see that being a gay or lesbian person is not hidden in the least. Anchor people and professional people in all walks of life proudly advertise their sexual preference and behavior everyday. We have a female police chief in Asheville, North Carolina that is rumored to belong to the lickity split club and it doesn't affect her job at all. She's a good looking female and no doubt brings out that lesbian feeling in a lot of admiring men. One thing for sure if people used their heads more we wouldn't have such a population explosion threatening the entire planet. I've predicted for years that the human species will eventually screw ourselves out of existence and we're well on our way of doing it. For the large part human beings are basically nimble brained creatures that can only think of here and now.

I don't know about everyone else but I'm sick and tired of paying taxes with money that I don't have while half the country sits on their lazy give me something else ass and pays no taxes at all you can always depend on those assholes to protest about everything and start a riot. They feel empowered by wearing black clothes and a mask as they destroy someone else's property and assault people with clubs. It's obvious that most are democrats and still pissed off because crooked Hillary lost the election. At protest they love waving a black flag like isis does because they stand for the same thing. They formed an organization which they call "antifa" which is made up of street thugs and people that want more free stuff from the government. Look at "planned parenthood." they expect the people that pay taxes to pay for them screwing their brains out and getting knocked up. It seems like all of the "cum receptacles" end up there for an abortion that they don't have to pay for. In the past planned parenthood even admitted to selling baby parts from performed abortions which they were proud of according to one under cover video shown on television. They x-ray one tit to justify murdering unborn babies and selling their body parts.

Look at congress and watch five hundred thirty five self centered ass-holes running around with their heads up their ass trying to recycle into something useful. Almost all of them are lawyers and that should tell you something. Every lawyer that I've ever had to deal with turned out to be a money hungry back stabbing son of a bitch. I had to deal with two judges that were obviously mentally handicapped and unfit to be a judge. Neither one knew their ass from a hole in the ground and couldn't find their ass with both hands and a map like most of the lawyers I've known. The simple and only explanation that I can come up with is that they attended some jerk ass law school and majored in stupidity one-o-one. People should realize that as long as lawyers run our government the country will remain in chaos. I always hear some flaming ass liberal tell people how people and especially children are dying on the streets from lack of care and starvation. Have you ever heard such bullshit? I have yet to find one person dead on the street from starvation and our country is flowing over with fat ass people living on government issued food stamps.

As soon as a Mexican or anyone else climbs over the fence to get into America they immediately apply and get all forms of welfare including food stamps. Most of the fence climbers or train riders get knocked up in Mexico and comes to America to squirt out their babies and pick up some welfare. Having the babies doesn't cost them a dime and the first thing that they start yelling is "don't deport me and split up our family." as far as I'm concerned I say deport her fat illegal ass and send all the kids back with her. That way we can't be accused of splitting up her family. That way her lover can knock her up again in Mexico.

Like I've said before, I'm sick and tired of being white and being blamed for everything. I hope the hell when I wake up in the morning I'm black, brown, yellow, green or anything but white. I want on the gravy train too and get all the free shit without having to work. I want to be able to sit on my ass all day too and get drunk on my ass every Saturday night. Hopefully I'll be black because I want to know what it feels like to kick some white dude's ass. I won't have to worry about buying a new television set when mine wears out. I'll join a protest, break out the window at an appliance store and pick myself out a brand new flat screen television set that I can carry home in my stolen car. Man, that's living and I had to waste so much of my life being white.

There are politically correct forces active today that have set out to completely destroy southern heritage. Former South Carolina Governor Nikki Haley, started the trend of destroying southern heritage by removing the Confederate flag from the front of the state capitol in Columbia. You really caved in to the radicals and I hope you realize what you started. The liberal left and radicals had a statue of Robert E Lee removed in Virginia and have set out to rename everything that refers to the old south. These people are completely ignorant of the causes that forced the south to secede from the union. The largest slave market in the united states was in New York City and the Confederate flag never flew over one slave ship. Southern people never went to Africa and put blacks into chains. They didn't open slave markets and sell slaves. Putting blacks into chains and making a business out of selling slaves was a creation of northern people. Buying blacks from the tribal chiefs in Africa and putting them in chains to be sold to southern plantation owners was a thriving business for northern slave traders. In route back to America from Africa with a shipload of slaves it was common practice to throw any slave overboard that was causing trouble. That was the way the ship's master would resolve any on board problem. So all you people that blame southern people for bringing poor black people to America against their will can place the blame where it belongs.

It's a shame that so many people are ignorant regarding the civil war and the history of General Lee. One real dumb asshole that stands out above the others is ex-vice President, Joe Biden. When he went to make a speech before the NAACP the first thing he said was "the Republican Party will put you back into chains." this was the height of plain stupidity made by a jerk that said on national television twice that Obama was not qualified to be President of the united states during the democratic nomination process. In my opinion and after observing his bizarre way of thinking I'm convinced he's fighting senility. Between him, Obama and his cronies they almost destroyed our country. They pissed around with North Korea until that moron leader has shown that he is capable of hitting America with nuclear weapons. Between Bush, Clinton and Obama's program of appeasement toward North Korea they have left President Trump with the problem that they should have resolved. When and if that moron drops a bomb on Los Angeles or New York City the liberal left will take their heads out of their ass and support President Trump's efforts.

Instead of the black people bashing white southerners they should be appreciative and give thanks for all the white southerners that gave their lives fighting Hitler during world war two. If Hitler had won the war he would have made stove wood out of the entire black race. If you think he hated the Jewish people it doesn't even start to compare what he thought of the black race. So before you start bashing and bad mouthing white southern people, take history into account. It bewilders me how blacks usually always vote the democratic ticket and supports the party that enslaved them. For some unknown reason unless it's just ignorance and stupidity, they always support the democrat running for office. Just look at the mayor of Chicago, Rahm Emanuel, he has got to be the dumbest idiot around. Of course that figures because he came out of the Obama administration before becoming mayor of Chicago. Between this jerk and Eric Holder, who use to be Obama's attorney general, no wonder America went to hell in a handbasket. Hopefully things will start to improve since we got rid of those morons that didn't know their ass from a hole in the ground.

Some people probably believe that the practice of slavery just came into being. It would surprise the hell out of them to know that slavery has been around for a thousand years. Do they think that the great pyramids of Egypt were constructed by upper class Egyptians? In colonial times slavery was a big money making enterprise started by northern ship owners. The going selling price for a healthy worthwhile slave was fifteen hundred dollars which was a small fortune during those times. The south's survival depended on agriculture and northern ship owners saw a potential gold mine in providing slaves for southern plantation owners. It became a big time business completely monopolized in New York and almost every slave ship was docked in Massachusetts. You can rest assured that plantation owners provided better living conditions to the slaves then what they had in Africa. It was incumbent upon slave owners to take care of them the best they could because they represented a huge investment that they couldn't afford to lose. I personally don't endorse or support any form of slavery because it was truly a case of cruelty. Tribal chiefs tearing them away from other family members and placing them in chains had to be terrible and cruel at least in America they were provided with the basic needs of food, clothing and shelter. Even that doesn't justify being placed into slavery and being owned by someone. That was a sad chapter in America, but in retrospect it was a blessing in disguise for the black people. If it hadn't been for slavery millions of blacks here now in America would probably be in Africa living in squalor.

The thirteen southern states making up the confederacy was the country of my ancestors and I hold no shame being southern born and bred. I know that any form of slavery is wrong, but right now considering my health and financial status 1 could really use one or two of them to get me through this part of my troubled life. I suppose everyone has their share of problems as in the case of my personal physician. One day I was being examined by him after he had just examined another patient. As I was lying on the examination table I overheard the receptionist call the doctor on the intercom system and tell him that the patient he had just examined had suddenly dropped dead on the floor as he was leaving the waiting area. The doctor thought for a few seconds and then told the receptionist to turn him around so it would look like he was just coming in instead of leaving. The doctor made a wise decision otherwise he'd have half a dozen lawyers filing lawsuits against him for malpractice. Everyone knows that if a person simply farts in the presence of a lawyer they can expect to be sued and have the full force of the environmental protection agency brought down on them. Don't laugh I did less then that and had to pay out one hundred twenty five thousand dollars to some trailer trash freeloaders which I explained in the book "Kangaroo Justice."

The political correct crowd is making every effort to delete God and religion from our lives and it surprises me that they haven't started filing lawsuits and hammering on our national motto "in God we trust." it must make them sick to see it printed on all our currency. Madelyn O'Hare, the mother of all atheist must roll over in her miserable grave knowing that God is still around in spite of her efforts to get rid of him. The loss of all her gold and her death served the miserable fat bitch right. Hopefully the fat bitch is burning in hell with the rest of her sorry ass friends. I've learned a few things in life and wish the hell I could have learned more. When men and women get married they act like a couple of love birds. Two years later they fight like hell and can't stand each other. It's really funny. When they get married the man thinks that his wife will stay the same and the woman thinks that she can change her husband. That's love for you, it can be blind as hell and you don't realize it until it's too late.

Nothing is as it seems on the surface and people lose the art of understanding a simple communication. A couple examples come to mind. The first regards something that happened to me when I went into my favorite watering hole for a beer. I took a seat at the counter, ordered a beer and started eating from a bowl of nuts on the counter top. A good looking young woman came into the bar and sat down next to me and ordered a beer. As she got her beer I pushed the bowl over to her and asked her if she'd like to eat my nuts and that's how the fight got started. I was just trying to be friendly and share the bowl of nuts with her and she took it the wrong way. Case number two is just another example of how people lose communication skills. Three men were sitting in the waiting room of a urologist physician to be examined for the same problem. One patient had red testicles, one patient had green testicles and the third patient had brown testicles. The doctor examined the patient with the red testicles first. When the patient paid for the examination the receptionist charged him twenty five dollars. The doctor then examined the patient with the green testicles and when he went to pay for the examination the receptionist charged him two hundred dollars. At this the patient blew up and became completely irate asking the receptionist why did she only charged the patient with red testicles only twenty five dollars and charging him two hundred dollars? The receptionist explained to him that there is a big difference between lipstick and gangrene. After all three of them were examined the patient with the brown testicles went home. When he got home and went into the house all he could see was a sink full of dirty dishes, clothes on the floor and the bed wasn't even made up. He told his wife just look at the mess and what the hell have you been doing all day? She got upset and told him that she's been so busy with the kids all day that she hasn't had time to wipe her ass. With this he said, yes and that's something else I want to talk to you about.

Sometimes it seems that I've just about lost all my compassion for human beings. I worry more about the welfare of my pets then I do of any neighbor. I donate money every month to at least six different organizations that save and protect animals. Until you have felt the love and devotion of a little puppy you haven't lived. Looking at the problems I have had with my neighbors the majority of human beings disgust the hell out of me and the rest seem to have no purpose either.

Between ignorant citizens, bitchy neighbors and money grubbing lawyers I prefer to be left alone. A perfect example of how screwed up our country is just look at congress. They stay in office until they become senile and steal everything they can get their hands on. The only way we can get the bums out of office is to have term limits. With term limits maybe we can save our country before those idiots completely destroy it. Everywhere you look you'll find some loud mouth racist shooting off their mouth. Take Maxine Pottymouth for example, she's nothing but a typical loud mouth racist and she's ugly as hell on top of that. People keep voting her back into office which shows their ignorance. Another thing that really burns my ass is how black people in congress will form different organizations within the various corners of government comprised of only blacks. They have their own colleges as in the case of Florida memorial college in north Dade County, Florida. In the Dade County Sheriff's Office the blacks created the "progressive officers club" comprised of the black officers on the department. Anytime anyone uses the term progressive, it signifies a radical movement of some kind and you can expect lawsuits to be coming down the pike. In that particular case they were setting the groundwork to approach the "equal opportunity commission" and complain that the department didn't have enough blacks in upper management positions. Of course the department caved in as usual and gave them anything they demanded. The black officers took a page out of the book of the "black caucus" organization in congress that promotes their own agenda and particular interest in government. Then the black officers created "noble" in various police departments to further their own personal interest in the departments. Of course the NAACP has been around for years sticking their nose into everything that involves a black. Take "affirmative action" for instance which is nothing but reverse discrimination. The liberals called it giving minorities a "level playing ground" which was nothing but a lot of bullshit. They've had the level playing field now for forty years and even with discrimination on their side they're still in the same place complaining constantly about everything. Companies, universities and business opportunities of every kind have discriminated against white people for years and the time for the so-call level playing field has to end. It's high time for white people to have an equal opportunity and not be discriminated against any longer. How long does the liberal bleeding hearts and racist black organizations need to continually punish the white race? If it continues over time they will create a Frankenstein monster that they won't be able to control and deal with. Then all of them will stand around scratching their ass wondering what happened.

It reminds me of the book that crooked Hillary just wrote entitled "What Happened." She blames everyone for her losing the presidential election except herself. It was almost common knowledge that she and her husband "Slick Willy" was crooked as hell even dating back to when he was governor of Arkansas and involved in the "White Water" scandal Hillary is so crooked they'll have to screw her into the ground when she finally dies. I always knew that Washington, D.C. was run and controlled by crooked politicians and lawyers, but I never dreamed that the corruption ran so deep. President Trump was correct when he called it a sewer because it's totally gutted with self serving lawyers. The republican senators in congress have abandoned President Trump in his effort to get anything accomplished. I'm a strong republican, but I hope the hell senators like John McCain, Jeff Flake, Collins, and Makowski lose their seat in the next election. I remember Senator Grahm saying on national television that he hopes everyone tells Trump to go to hell Senator John McCain, shows his jealousy toward President Trump because he lost his bid to be President and Trump didn't. John McCain is a republican in name only because he does everything he can to see that President Trump fails. Senator McCain should do us all a favor and join the Democratic Party which he supports. Hopefully Jeff Flake and John McCain will be voted out of office in the next election.

Senator McCain, makes a moving speech before the senate telling everyone how they should unite and do the people's work. Then a couple days later he turns around and votes no to stop the republican effort to replace Obamacare. A real example of party dedication, huh? I always hear people talking about freedom of speech and how the American people can enjoy so much freedom. Hell, we have the freedom to riot, destroy property, burn the American flag, disrupt public meetings, rob, steal, assault and kill with total disregard of the law and it goes on and on. If that's the freedom you endorse then go for it, but my love and devotion regarding freedom is quite different. Quite frankly I personally feel that we have too much freedom in our country. Burning and stomping on the American flag should get you arrested and a good ass kicking by the roadside on your way to the jailhouse. I totally agree with Vladimir Putin of Russia when he stated that everyone wasn't entitled to a trial if the police observe a person committing a crime and catch him in the act, why the hell should that person be entitled to a trial and waste taxpayers money? Just sentence him and throw his sorry ass into jail for the duration. We have freedom coming out of our ears in our country to the point that it's ridiculous. We're so concerned with protecting a person that when an officer arrest someone the first thing he is obligated to do is advise the person not to say anything. Advise him that he has Miranda rights and doesn't have to say anything and can tell the officer to go to hell if he feels like it. To me, this is the height of stupidity and the officer has to let the person know that he's entitled to a lawyer and if he can't afford one the state will give him one. The officer has to inform the person that anything he says will be held against him in court. With the Miranda rights even a retarded moron would know better then to say a word. When the officer is finally done advising him of all his rights he has to ask the person if he understands what he's been told? If the arrested person says anything he must be flat out stupid as hell or completely brain dead.

I was sued by a fat ass lying bitch lawyer in south Florida and had to pay a trailer trash couple one hundred twenty five thousand dollars for producing and distributing hundreds of slanderous posters with my wife's picture all over the county. To really understand the true meaning of trash and how a lying lawyer can rob you, read the book "Kangaroo Justice." I've never met a lawyer yet that couldn't put John Dillinger to shame when it comes to robbing someone and they do it without a gun. All of them have a license to steal and they are experts at it with no shame. Sometimes I just feel like giving up. It seems like the wealthy people have all the luck and things always goes south with us poor slobs. Well to do people are offered millions of dollars to write a book of their boring lives and I'd feel lucky if I was offered ten dollars. In order for me to write a book and have it published I have to borrow whatever I need on a credit card. I have to do it because it's the only way I can get my side of the disgusting story of robbery out for the public to see. Take crooked Hillary for example, if you want a signed book of hers with a picture of her it will cost you two thousand four hundred dollars. I'll consider myself lucky if I can get two dollars and forty cents. That's the difference between being rich and being poor I suppose. I hear that ex director of the FBI, James Comey, has been offered two million dollars to write a book and you can rest assured it certainly won't cover any of his crooked dealings. He was probably born with a silver spoon stuck in his mouth like most of the other well dressed thieves in politics. I wonder how many of them lived in poverty and experienced having nothing. I was born in a small town in northern Alabama in an old farm house that looked like it was about to fall down at any time. The umbilical cord had wrapped itself around my neck and I was born almost dead. My life was saved by an old country doctor that put breath back into my little lungs. My mother told me when I was old enough to understand that it was obvious that the Lord had put me on earth for some special reason. It was never revealed to me why my life was saved and if the Lord ever thought that I was special.

My family was dirt poor and my mother made my clothes out of flour sacks, but every stitch had my mother's love. Even the main road in town was a gravel and dirt road with wooden sidewalks. If I told you how and what we had to do to survive such poverty you'd wonder how the hell any of us survived. There were nine of us in the family including my parents and I'm the only one left. I'm just a crippled old man and I suppose the most I ever accomplished in life was just staying alive. I bought myself a grave plot, a funeral and a headstone because I know that I'm living the twilight years of my life and time is running out. Sometimes I go to the cemetery and put flowers on my grave site just to see what it will look like when I'm gone from this life. Who else do you know that has the privilege of decorating their own grave site? My wife and I drive a worn out twenty one year old truck with three hundred thousand miles on it. I thought for sure that someday we could buy a better vehicle to drive, but the lawsuit against me destroyed that dream for good. The lawyer and the trailer trash might have destroyed me of ever getting to own and riding in a nice vehicle for the time being. Someday I'll get to ride in a nice new hearse to the cemetery and there's no way they can deny me that.

The only hope of me ever getting back on my feet before I die depends on marketing my book. I've lived enough poverty in my life and don't want anymore of it. I've had to work for everything I have and thought I had saved enough to last me for the rest of my life, but the trailer trash and a lying lawyer stripped me of everything I had saved and more. I had to place a mortgage on my home in such an amount that I will never be able to pay it off before I die. Hopefully all of them will die, rot and burn in hell for what they have done to what life I have left. My life has been destroyed because of them producing and distributing hundreds of slanderous posters with my wife's picture all over the county and on the front door of our church house. That's right and you didn't misunderstand me. I had to pay that trailer trash a fortune for slandering my family. Sometimes I see someone on television stating that they forgive the person for killing a family member of theirs. Well, I'm not so forgiving and have always felt that a surviving family member should have the right and opportunity to execute anyone that has been convicted of murdering a member of another family. Proper punishment for any murderer should be drawn and quartered by horses for everyone to see. That's exactly what should have happened to that murdering scumbag O.J. Simpson. Why Mr. Goldman never found an opportunity to blow Simpson's rotten brains out is beyond me. I don't like violence because I'm basically a peaceable man, but seeing how society is now I took it on myself to buy a handgun to carry on myself for protection. If someone or a bunch of punk democrats attempt to drag me out of my vehicle because they don't like my Trump sticker they had better be bullet proof. I won't hesitate for a second to shoot someone's ass off if I'm assaulted because I'm too old to get my ass kicked and too young to die. It wouldn't bother me in the least if I was convicted for killing some sorry son of a bitch and sentenced to twenty years because according to nature the end of my life is just around the corner.

The more I think of my career as a police officer the more I regret not kicking more ass and applying roadside justice when it was so badly needed. One early morning as I was riding the prowl car I caught a prowler coming out from between two houses in a residential section. As he crossed a vacant lot to get to his parked car I stopped him and inquired what he was doing between houses at three a.m. in the morning. When I asked for his identification it turned out that he was a lawyer and a real smart ass lawyer at that. As soon as he handed me his drivers license he asked for it back and informed me that I had it for an unreasonable length of time. It was obvious that he didn't want me to make note of his name or check him through communications. It crossed my mind to kick his smart ass and adjust his attitude which I didn't do and still regret to this day. I did obtain his telephone number and made a point of calling his house, waking his wife up and informing her that I had her husband and asked her if she knew why he was out prowling around at three a.m. in the morning? Hearing her screaming over the telephone gave me a lot more pleasure then kicking his smart ass. Let's face it. There are some people that are so stupid and thick headed they need a good ass kicking every now and then to get their head back on straight and to adjust their attitude.

I took part in the Nineteen Sixty Eight riots in Miami, Florida and realized that rioters for the most part have an intelligence level of an imbecile or lower. During the rioting they threw gasoline on a car occupied by an elderly white couple and lit it on fire. Two young men that knew nothing about the rioting on north west sixty second street drove into the riot and were dragged out of their car and stomped simply because they were white. After stomping them the rioters got into the victim's car and drove back and forth over one of them. They continued driving back and forth over him until he was mashed and torn apart all over the street. We had the authority and should have been given permission to shoot the animals before the victims were murdered. No, let me correct myself, the rioters weren't near as good as animals. Calling a rioter an animal is an injustice to the animal world. After the riot you will always hear the racist Maxine Pottymouth of California shooting her mouth off about how the rioters were treated. Of course you'll always hear that skinny little runt, Al Pimpton, shooting his racist mouth off too. Regarding Maxine Pottymouth, I still can't figure out how she can own mansions all over California on her one hundred seventy four thousand dollar government salary. That loud mouth bitch has never felt anyones pain and you'd think by now they would be able to see what she really is. The people that keep voting her into office have to be completely blind and ignorant. Besides being ugly as hell she leads her supporters around like sheep. It would be interesting to know where and how she gets all her money to be able to live so high on the hog so to speak. One thing for sure she knows how to work a crowd of ignorant people as good as hairlip Jesse Fraction or the little skinny little peep squeak, Al Pimpton. Have you noticed lately how those two con artist have dropped out of sight?

Someday it wouldn't surprise me if the truth finally comes out regarding the actual birth place of Obama. Doesn't it make you wonder why his college records remain sealed from the public? People that attended the same schools and majored in the same subjects never seen him in any classes. Best yet, not one female has ever stepped forward and said that she ever dated him or even knew him. It doesn't take a rocket scientist to figure out that he must belong to one of the groups in the LGBT crowd. The only picture I ever saw of him when he was claiming to be in Hawaii was him sitting on his ass smoking what appeared to be a joint. As President he made one speech after the other praising the koran and the muslim faith. He travelled the world apologizing for America and it certainly showed where his allegiance was and it certainly wasn't America. You would think with his money he'd at least help his father financially who lives in squalor overseas. Obama has ruined the prospects of another black person ever being elected President of the united states. Obama was such a sorry ass empty suit I find it hard to believe that enough voters would take the chance on another black person. Of course knowing the intellect of voters it wouldn't surprise me if the Democratic Party nominated Maxine Pottymouth to run for President. I'm not an authority, but it's obvious that she doesn't have both oars in the water. I worked with mentally ill people for four years and I can recognize a screwball in short order.

Bernie Oddball is another screwball that runs short on brain matter. That moron prides himself for being a socialist and attracted a lot of support from young people because they know that every socialist will always give free stuff away until they run out of other people's money. Venezuela is an example of a socialist government gone to hell and you won't see Bernie Oddball saying anything about what has happened to that government. That's the kind of government that good ole Bernie thinks we need , so say something Bernie. He's just another sheep herder like most other liberal democrats so why should we be surprised by anything he does? He's another one that should have had his ass kicked on the roadside a long time ago. As a young boy, I like all the other young kids would occasionally demonstrate a total lack of judgment and common sense. During that time in my life I exhibited a degree of cruelty to the animal world that I've regretted for the last seventy years and have asked the Lord's forgiveness for my brainless behavior. Even though some people called hunting a sport I soon realized that killing animals was wrong and they had just as much right to live as any other creature on earth including human beings. I promised the Lord that 1 would spend the rest of my life taking care of all animals and until this day I always donate money to any and every organization that shelters and protects animals. There is no limit to what I'll spend to save a poor sick or injured animal one day on a cold winter day I found a poor little kitten in a snowbank that someone dropped off because he was unwanted. I saved that little fellow and raised him for seven years giving him the best possible and loving home that I could. Unfortunately he developed heart trouble and I spent over four thousand dollars trying to save him to no avail after working around and being with human beings for years, I place my love and devotion for animals far over my compassion for most human beings. Anyone that observes human behavior toward other humans will no doubt come to the same conclusion. Anyone that comes to my house might for some reason slap me around and be mean, but one thing for sure they had better not abuse and hurt one of my pets. My pets are valid members of my family that can't defend themselves so I'll never hesitate for one second to do it for them. I'm one of those people that prefer to be left alone and stay to myself.

When I write I only write about true life experiences and not a figment of my imagination. The only way I have to tell my side of the story is to write a book because I don't have a forum on some television show to reach millions of people. I'm just a poor slob that got robbed by crooked lawyers and a couple dumb ass judges. To really get the picture on how you can get robbed by the myth of due process, read the book entitled "Kangaroo Justice and how well dressed thieves have a license to steal." always bear in mind that a judge is just another lawyer who is completely impressed with himself even though he may be the dumbest asshole in the courtroom. Just because a person is a judge doesn't mean that he knows his ass from a hole in the ground. 1 see where ex-FBI director James Comey, was offered two million dollars to write a book. Maybe John Dillinger and Al Capone should have written a book too. It's common knowledge that Comey was in the pockets of Loretta Lynch, the attorney general and Numerous morons. Loretta lynch, advised him to refer to the Hillary investigation as a matter and refrain from saying that it was an investigation. So now it's known as the federal bureau of matters. Maybe Comey can now explain why Hillary had her blackberry and other electronic devices smashed with a hammer even after they were subpoenaed. Maybe he can explain what Hillary did with thirty thousand missing e-mails that were also under subpoena. With all of that Comey had the balls to state that there wasn't enough evidence to indict Hillary's lying ass. Go ahead and write a book Comey, and tell us all about it. Every time he opens his mouth his nose grows a little more. I can always tell when he's lying because his jaw moves. It wasn't his job to tell the attorney general who should or shouldn't be prosecuted, but that little fact didn't stop him. Of course I'm sure he'll explain why the attorney general Loretta Lynch, met Bill Clinton on the tar mack for thirty nine minutes in privacy to discuss their kids. Hillary is under investigation and Bill is meeting with the attorney general to discuss their children. Talk about the fix being in, a retard with an I.Q. of ten would know better. Anyone believing that explanation has to belong to the Obama administration or the Democratic Party in some fashion. There seems to be no end to Comey's bizarre behavior and I suppose you have to be crooked to a degree to have anyone offer you two million dollars to write a book. Hell, I'll write a book on any subject if someone will get all my money back that was stolen from me. Two million is a lot of money and I'd be thankful and feel lucky as hell if I was offered two dollars. When people stomp on you and lie about you it's hard to take and you start looking for any avenue for pay back. Writing is the only possible way a poor slob can pay back to the trailer trash, lying lawyers and dumb ass judges that swim daily in the septic tank of life. It has gotten to the point that the sorry bastards can't hurt me anymore then they already have. I have come to realize how a person can be pushed to the point of acute vengeance. The bastards have gotten robbery down and perfected that they don't even need a gun. Every time I see a lawyer all I can see is a big pile of dung. It's a shame that the government outlawed dueling because it was such a good and effective way of getting rid of trash. It's a great way of settling your differences with intellectual trash instead of having to go to court and putting up with some lying lawyer and brain dead judge. Looking at human behavior it convinces me that there are a lot of people that need to be laid to rest to improve society. The premise that everyone is entitled to a trial is a lot of baloney as far as I'm concerned. A murderer caught holding a victim's head in his hands sure as hell doesn't deserve a trial and having four or five lawyers doing everything they can possibly do to get him found not guilty and set free to do it again. It's common knowledge that lawyers don't give a rat's ass about the guilt or innocence of a defendant. I've testified in enough trials to understand how lawyers think. Most of them represents the scum of society until it becomes hard to tell the difference between them. William Shakespeare, had the right idea many years ago when he said that they should be rounded up and gotten rid of. I don't have to strain my imagination to wonder how most divorce lawyers are compensated for their legal services. I know how that works because when I was in the traffic section on the department enforcing traffic laws it was common to be offered something other than money to overlook a traffic violation. I never felt at ease writing a female a ticket because I knew that if she was upset she was potential trouble. On one occasion on north Miami Beach Blvd I stopped a female driver for obstructing traffic and not yielding to oncoming traffic. As soon as I stopped her I knew by her attitude that I was going to have a handful of trouble because she started using profanity that I would only expect from a drunk sailor. She tried everything in her effort to get out of the ticket and when that failed she started yelling that I had touched her and started asking people walking down the sidewalk for their names so they could be witnesses against me. My first thought was to arrest her for disorderly conduct because it was obvious that she was a nut job and should be committed into the hospital for evaluation. I requested a supervisor to respond to my location because it had gotten out of hand. Luckily I had stopped her in front of a bar and everyone in the bar came outside to see what the commotion was all about. Looking back on the incident I should have arrested her, but instead I gave her the ticket and let her go on her way. The very next day that loud mouth sorry bitch went to the department's internal affairs section and made a complaint against me stating that I tried to take her to her house for sex and when she refused I issued her the traffic ticket. When the internal affairs officer investigated the incident and saw how ugly and old she was he dismissed the complaint because he knew that I couldn't possibly be that hard up. All the bar patrons present that day were interviewed and stated that I didn't do or say anything out of the way and should have arrested the woman.

When I was a young man growing up in Miami, Florida, I was only aware of the Miami police department. There were two motorcycle officers that always had my attention and respect, officers Paul Dixon and Charley Cox. I was young and a little on the stupid side like most other teenagers, especially racing around town on our motorcycles. I'll never forget the day that Officer Dixon, rode by my house on his beautiful shiney police bike and happened to see me standing in my front yard with some of my rowdy friends. He turned around and stopped next to us and told us that all of the hell raising with our motorcycle club had to stop or he was going to start making arrest. Being a little smart ass and trying to impress my friends I told him that he couldn't arrest me because I wasn't doing anything. He told me that he'd think of a charge on the way to the jail house. I loved his response and attitude and decided right then that someday I was going to be a motorcycle officer just like him. His uniform, demeanor and police bike placed me in awe and I couldn't wait to become twenty one years of age and apply for the Miami Police Department.

Boy, did I ever get the surprise and disappointment of my life. When I turned twenty one years of age and went to the police department to apply for the job which I had waited so long for, I was turned down for being one quarter of an inch too short in height. I couldn't believe such bad luck because these days they will hire almost anyone. You can be under twenty one years of age, a borderline midget, illiterate and they'll still hire you. As time passed I decided to apply at the Dade County Sheriff's Office for a police position where you had to be at least five foot nine inches tall in your stocking feet. I saw officers skinny as a rail where their back pockets seemed to be joined together. Physical strength and above average intelligence didn't seem to be that important. When I joined the Dade County Sheriff's Office I actually witnessed new applicants being taught how to read and write. The new hiring programs with the police departments really started to bug my ass big time. I was educated and reading and writing was certainly no problem and I was turned down for being one quarter of an inch too short in height. In their zeal to hire minorities they would hire anyone that could walk without dragging their knuckles on the ground. Being able to read and write wasn't that important as long as it was a minority. The departments ended up with a slew of unqualified morons that within a few years were given command positions not knowing their ass from a hole in the ground. I personally held numerous college degrees in the arts, criminal science and public administration which was about as useful as toilet paper with the department. With all of the degrees I had to work for supervisors that probably had to cheat their way through the sixth grade in elementary school the situation only got worse year after year and really fell into the sewer when the county commission decided to join the politically correct crowd and hired an empty suit county manager by the name of Merrit Steerass. He had affirmative action coming out of his ears and was determined to hire and promote every minority he could find in Liberty City, Brown Sub and Opa-Locka. The only thing he was interested in was skin color and any qualifications weren't even considered. He thought he was an expert on how to run a police department and decided to run off anyone that was a professional in police administration. He was such a sorry manager he would sneak out the back stairway of the courthouse at quitting time so as not to be seen by anyone. Hopefully, that sorry bastard didn't go to another police department and destroy it after he left Dade County. I don't have any idea how that jerk ever got any deserved respect from anyone. In retrospect, I wish I had dated his secretary and made the director of the police department. Of all the people needing a good old time ass kicking by the roadside it was him.

When I was just a skinny little kid on our farm in northern Alabama I never realized that we were poor people. At Christmas time I never received any toys like other kids. My Christmas gift was a sack of oranges, apples and various nuts. One Christmas my dad brought us kids two beautiful little puppies that we named Right and Left. We were as happy as we could be and those two little puppies brought us happiness beyond description. We all had such a beautiful Christmas sitting in front of the fireplace and hearing our mother thanking the Lord for all her children. Our family never owned a car or even a bicycle. We had an old broken down mule and a sad old wagon that she would pull to the church every Sunday morning. No one ever laughed at us because they knew that we were poor and looking back it seems like everyone in town was poor and scratching for a living. There was no electricity in town to speak of and I always had a hard time staying awake in church on Sunday night. The only light in church was from kerosene lanterns placed along the walls. It was always so dim in the church house it was hard not to fall asleep. The preacher never hesitated to wake me up by announcing it from the pulpit as he preached. We always walked to the church on Sunday nights and it was so dark the only way you'd know that you were walking off the paved roadway was by hearing the crunching of the gravel on the side of the roadway. None of the homes had electricity and kerosene lamps were your only source of light. There was no such thing as indoor plumbing and restroom facilities was a slop jar. I have to laugh when ! Hear young people these days complain about how hard they have it. They have no idea what hard times are and probably consider it hard times if they don't have a car to drive or a nice big allowance from their parents so they can go and eat in some high class restaurant. In Alabama my sisters would go out into the woods and find some polk salad to pick and my older brothers would go and find a rabbit or squirrel for the dinner table. If it wasn't for rabbits and polk salad we would probably have starved. I came into this world with nothing and it looks like that's the way I'm going to leave it.

If you don't remember anything else there's one thing you should always bear in mind. All the material things that you have acquired in your life time is only yours temporarily. You can't take it with you and when you die someone else will own your pretty house, car and property, so enjoy it while you can.

We lived in such an old farm house that every time there was a storm and especially at night my mom would round us all up and make a run to the storm shelter which was a cave in a large bank across from our house. My dad dug the cave and installed a heavy wooden door for protection. When we took shelter in it we'd stay all night with a kerosene lantern and some blankets. We'd always stay all night because my mom was afraid that our house would fall down in the high wind. I slept many nights on a bench listening to the door shake and the high wind outside. Sometimes to this day I feel like bad times have never been so bad and I find myself fighting depression all alone. Yes, strong and old men do cry at times. They just do it when they're all alone and no one can see them.

I know that I'm a victim of weakness because I violate the Lord's third commandment too often which I'm truly sorry. Hopefully someday I'll find some peace in my valley and be worthy of saving. I've seen and experienced so much hardship and heart break in my life that it has made me lose compassion for other people. I hope it never happens to you, but someday you might find yourself a crippled old man through no fault of your own. After life has hammered and beaten you down rest assured your outlook at life and death will change. You'll begin to realize that death is part of life and it won't seem to be so grim anymore.

In the book "Kangaroo Justice" it's explained how I got robbed of my entire savings and more by a lying lawyer and two brain dead judges that had no idea or intention of administering justice. All three are a disgrace to the judicial system of justice and hopefully one day they will have to stand good for what they have done to me. Who knows, maybe someday a worthwhile lawyer who actually believes in the concept of due process will learn of my robbery and appeal the unlawful decisions of the courts and get my money back before I'm planted in the cemetery. What happened to my wife and I is unbelievable, but rest assured it's a true story. In desperation I hired a lawyer that advertised twenty five years of experience. I learned too late that he probably had twenty five years of experience throwing people underneath the bus. During my experience with so-called due process I discovered that lawyers and judges are cut from the same cloth and will make any ruling to protect another lawyer's back. I've testified hundreds of times in every kind of court but never recognized such ignorance as in the south Florida court and the superior court in Asheville, North Carolina. The female lawyer, douche bag Mary, that operates out of the fat, dumb and happy law firm on West Broward Blvd. isn't stupid because she has robbing someone down to a science. Maybe she isn't stupid in the sense of understanding the difference between the truth and a lie. She has never had any problem swearing a lie before any court and having a judge accept it. Makes me wonder if there's something else between them if you get my drift. I spent twenty five years in law enforcement and she is the biggest liar that I've ever encountered. No doubt she has always been rejected by men including her husband due to her fat ass and ugly general appearance. She looks for dumb ass clients that will just sit on their ass and sign papers for her not having any idea what they're signing. One day that sorry bitch will turn around and I'll be standing there for her. At that moment she will realize that she's going to stand good for what she has done to my life. Study my case of robbery in the book "Kangaroo Justice" and you will understand my undying contempt for lawyers and judges. Kicking her sorry fat ass on the roadside would have given me a tremendous and deserving amount of pleasure and might have made her a better person if that's possible which I doubt.

Don't ever get too snug and comfortable in your surroundings because you might screw up like I did. I sold a beautiful home sitting on a hill top with five and a half acres with no nearby neighbors, to build and move into a restricted development. Looking back on that decision it became clear to me that I had jumped from the frying pan into the fire. I constructed a beautiful two story plantation style house on three and a half acres and discovered too late that my neighbors were still living in the past years and displayed an ignorance of retarded people. Anytime I ever did anything to our property a neighbor would immediately start bitching about it. I planted some trees and a neighbor bitched about it. I installed two small light poles with sixty watt bulbs and another neighbor bitched about it. He bitched about the two light poles that were two hundred feet from his house while he was installing twelve lights in his front yard. That particular neighbor thought that he was the high sheriff of the neighborhood and everyone was suppose to do as he said. In fact he was nothing but the neighborhood bully that was always trying to run over everyone else. Considering his bizarre behavior I'm convinced that he has a chemical imbalance and should be evaluated for a psychosis because he certainly doesn't think, act or talk in a normal fashion. The other neighbor next to me use to make me think that he was my friend, but he's totally pussy whipped by his wife and she runs the show. She sticks her nose into everyones business and objected to me flying my Confederate flag. She had her husband come to my house and tell me that the flag bothers her and she wanted it removed. I really liked her husband even though he had no balls. Apparently his wife grew a set of balls because she was wearing his pants to run their household. Since I refused to remove my flag she had her husband plant twenty five huge Leland trees next to our property in an effort to obstruct their view of my flag. I gave them a plat of the property showing that all the trees that they have planted are on a dedicated right of way leading to another neighbor's property which didn't mean anything to them. As far as they were concerned the dedicated roadway didn't mean jack shit to them. Their only interest was trying to hide my flag. When they had their cars covered with Obama stickers maybe I should have went to their house and ask them to remove them because they offended me and while they were at it to get rid of all their foreign cars too because they also offended me. They have two beautiful little boys that always waved at my wife and I whenever we passed their house. Now, if they see us coming down the street both of them will run and hide. We can't believe what they are doing to both their children by teaching them to hate. Children are not born with hate, it's a learned behavior and the parents are doing a great job teaching it to them. As far as I'm concerned both of those neighbors can go straight to hell and kiss my royal Canadian ass. All they do is bitch and if that's not bad enough let me tell you about the neighbor that owns some property across from us which is nothing but a big hole in the ground that they can't even give away. They've been trying to sell it for the past fifteen years and no one that has looked at it has ever expressed an interest in it. They live someplace miles from the development but always show up at the meetings to bitch about something. They admit that they have no intention of ever living in the development and don't want to give up their right to bitch. The wife is nothing but another fatso who thinks that she's Ma Barker and has put the word out that I don't know who I'm dealing with. Yes I do, you're just another fat and unattractive slob that thinks you're a bad ass. You run a business that's nothing more than a tax shelter for your husband's so-called construction company. I was in your kind of business long before you were ever born and I know how that kind of math works.

My wife and I have tried our best to be good neighbors to everyone and have finally realized that all of them are nothing but a bunch of pricks. I've always stayed out of other peoples business but fatso's state and federal income taxes reports must really be a work of art. The federal and state governments must wonder at times how a business can lose money year after year and be able to stay in business. Sounds like someone has discovered a way of avoiding income taxes. I understand that half the population doesn't pay any taxes at all and maybe they're in that half.

Now I see where Denmark has a program called "hug a terrorist." Well, I've got something they can hug and especially any jerk with a beard and wearing a diaper on his head which looks silly as hell.

I haven't seen that skinny little jerk, Al Pimpton, lately. He use to spend more time in the White House then Obama and now you can't even find the little jerk off. Someone told me the other day that they saw him on television shooting his mouth off again about something else and he looked old, tired and worn out. He has always had a bad case of diarrhea of the mouth. He was a very close advisor of President Obama and made over one hundred seventy six trips to the oval office to see him so I guess he just wore himself out.

Now we have some clown by the name of Zuckerberg, saying that the federal government should pay everyone a pay check for sitting on their ass and doing nothing. I understand that he's the unqualified chief executive officer at Facebook who gets a big salary for doing nothing but sitting on his lazy worthless ass. It's really funny as hell. Everyone has two or three lawyers that will sue your ass for the slightest reason. Right now the singer, Taylor Swift, is filing a lawsuit against some guy that touched her ass during an interview, so she claims. I'll bet ten dollars to a donut that she lost her virginity a long time ago and maybe she should sue that awful guy that punched a hole in that little membrane. Check out the blouse that she was wearing when she got so offended. She should have felt honored that the guy thought that her ass looked so good he couldn't control himself. If the guy really felt of her little ass then he should be ashamed of himself. If he was that damn horney, he should have had Mrs. Palm and her five daughters take care of him and satisfy his sexual urges. Manual oscillation of the penis is the best way of not knocking up a female and having to pay child support for eighteen years. Masturbating can be a lot of fun and it leaves you completely satisfied sexually. Of course you have to be careful because as a young boy I was taught that it will make you go blind. I've often wondered if there was any truth to that saying because in my older years I've noticed that my eyesight doesn't seem to be that good anymore.

Sometimes I just feel like giving up on life. It seems like when things start going wrong it never stops and it's just one mountain after the other. Every pet that I get and love so dearly always gets sick and dies. A lying bitch female lawyer and two brain dead judges have robbed me of my entire life savings and put me so far in debt that I will never be able to pay it off before I die. The lawyer that I hired to defend me told the opposing lawyers confidential information that I shared with him. Confidential information given to him was supposed to be privileged communication between a lawyer and his client and fall under the "code of silence" but that was something that my lawyer didn't recognize. He shared that information and it cost me the state protection law of "tenants by the entirety" which stated that each spouse owned one hundred percent of their property to prevent some lawyer from taking any of it in a lawsuit against either spouse. My lawyer and his loose mouth cost me one hundred twenty five thousand dollars. My vehicle is a twenty one year old truck with three hundred thousand miles on it and any dream of me ever owning a nice car has been smashed. On January fifteenth in twenty fifteen I had a back operation that left me a cripple.

People tell me to hang in there because things will get better. When I was a young man my mother would always told me when I was troubled, son things will always work out good for those that believe in and serve the Lord. Well mom, when do all the good things start to happen? Sometimes I feel like I have the weight of the world on my shoulders and could cry myself a river if I was only alone some place. I'm a God fearing man but I'm totally convinced that God has no control over a person's life and whatever happens to you whether good or bad is simply an accident of existence. Men are born with "free will" and performs acts to other people that's against everything the bible teaches us. If God controls everything then why does he permit a bus load of children on their way to Sunday school go over a cliff. Why was the Nazi party and Hitler permitted to murder millions of innocent people? If that wasn't bad enough then why was Joseph Stalin of Russia permitted to kill millions of innocent citizens? Everyday hundreds of people are robbed and murdered by other people who think nothing of it. Why does it happen? We'll never know, but sooner then not he'll be back and the world will know of his plan for mankind. Even the angels in heaven don't know when the Lord is going to return, but he will, bank on it. The one thing that really keeps me on a straight and narrow path is when he said deny me and I'll deny you before my father in heaven. I've noticed that most people fear death but death is part of life and no one should fear that part of life.

It looks like our country is completely screwed up and continually gets worse. Take the flaming ass liberal Rahm Emanuel, the mayor of Chicago. This idiot was part of the Obama administration which explains why he has his head up his ass. That moron invites and encourages illegal immigrants to come to Chicago and be welcomed with open arms. He has declared Chicago to be a sanctuary city for the safety of criminals. There's no end to this moron's sorry decision making process. To me he represents nothing more than a walking pile of feces. Then we have another asshole, the mayor of New York. He's just as sorry as Emanuel, and why either of them get voted into office is a blemish on the intelligence of the voters. The only explanation that I can think of for them being so ignorant is that both of them must be lawyers.

When I was a young person going to school every student was taught reading, writing and arithmetic it's my understanding now that students aren't even taught how to write anymore. For years on the department I observed police candidates coming on the department that couldn't read and write over a sixth grade level in elementary school it wouldn't be long before the forces of affirmative action would push them to the top and into command positions. Anytime you see any organization using the term "progressive" in their name it's because they intend to start pushing their racist agenda for blacks and other minorities to the front of the line. The black officers on the Dade County Sheriff's Office all got together and formed the "black progressive officer's club" and started complaining to everyone that would listen how they were being discriminated against by the department. They cried to the sheriff, the county manager, the county commission and to each other. It was determined that the black officers were having trouble passing the section on promotional exams entitled "reading comprehension" so that section was deleted from promotional exams. I suppose that was an attempt to level the playing field according to affirmative action. That didn't seem to result in the expected results so the entire written exam was dropped and the promotional process became a case of each applicant being interviewed and nothing else. Affirmative action and a real jerk of a county manager was all the "black progressive officer's club" needed to fill supervisory positions with their members on the department. It wasn't long before one of them was actually appointed to be the director of the department. In the sixties the department went so far to the extreme with corruption and favoritism to the degree that it resembled an organized criminal enterprise. They devised ways of eliminating trouble makers and anyone jeopardizing their security and exposing their operation. It got so bad that a local television station, WTVJ, set up cameras outside of their meeting places in some out of the way garage or building to record who was attending the clandestine meetings. On one occasion as they were recording a meeting from a van parked across the street a police captain who was attending the meeting walked up to the van and said, "I hope you're shooting it in color." A major's wife was seen at a local race track wearing a very expensive stolen bracelet which didn't seem to bother the major in the least. If you caused trouble the next day you would be stopped for a traffic violation, the trunk of your car searched and to your surprise it would be full of stolen property. You would be arrested and charged with possession of stolen property which would effectively end your police career and trouble making. It was not uncommon for the special enforcement unit to end someone's career in a more permanent fashion if it became necessary. The sad and tragic part of the special enforcement unit's actions is that the officers never realized that the individual that was being eliminated was set up and had to be gotten rid of to safe guard the security of the corrupt officers. Having someone murdered was a real simple thing to do. The special enforcement unit would be advised that information was obtained that a burglary was going to occur at a certain location and time. The information indicated that the person was known to be armed and dangerous. The special enforcement unit would go to the place that was going to be robbed and stake it out. The so-called intruder was told to go to the place late at night and meet someone of great importance who will give him instructions and share with him a pending heist that will make him rich. He was told that the door would be left unlocked for him and simply walk inside. When the unsuspecting trouble maker walked inside the only thing he heard or saw was a shotgun blast. He was dead as hell before he hit the floor and the problem was resolved. The corrupt officers gave a sigh of relief and the special enforcement unit got a commendation for a job well done.

Things were getting too hot and the major and his wife wearing the stolen bracelet left unannounced at night and moved to a little town in Georgia to avoid any investigations regarding his questionable criminal activities with the Dade County Sheriff's Office. We had our share of crooks on the department but the rank and file officers on the streets were honest, honorable and dedicated men who wouldn't hesitate to lay their life down for a citizen or another police officer. In my opinion too many of the crooked officers on the department got scott free of their crimes and never got prosecuted. I can say one thing for the Buncombe County sheriff's office in North Carolina. When any corruption was exposed in the sheriff's office by a public official they did something about it. When their elected sheriff got indicted, arrested and thrown into jail for his unlawful activities, there was no outcry or sympathy for him. He had developed a habit of spending and gambling with other people's money which didn't set too well with voters and county officials. Since then the voters have elected honorable men to serve as sheriff.

It's a shame that the Dade County leaders didn't cast a big enough net to catch all of the thieves when they had the chance to before all the crooks started leaving town. If it hadn't been for the news media they may never have been exposed and caught. The news media had them running like rats off a sinking ship. One went to a little town in Georgia, one went to North Carolina and tried to pass himself off as a retired police chief from Florida and the other one that I know of got hit and killed by a car as he was crossing the highway with a jug of whiskey. The ones that I knew of was only the tip of the iceberg.

After years of being a police officer and receiving very little respect I fully supported the concept of roadside justice being administered to some wise mouth and deserving punk. Sometimes that was the only justice being served because too many judges didn't have enough common sense to hit themselves on the ass with a bow fiddle. Some of the biggest asshole judges that I've ever run across even to this day make decisions that are only fitting for a moron. I personally have dealt with two judges that didn't give a tinkers damn about right and wrong. One in south Florida and one in Asheville, North Carolina. In the superior court in Asheville I had a lawyer claim that I was divorced and couldn't produce one document proving it. He testified that I had been divorced some years ago,. But didn't know where or when in his effort to have the court deny me the state law "tenants by the entirety" the judge acted like he wasn't even interested in finding out the truth and denied me the protection of "tenants by the entirety." the judge was wrong and I told him so and hopefully I'll live long enough to see the judge and the lawyer who robbed me stand good for what they've done.

I'm just a gun carrying, bible hugging southern gentleman. My national anthem is Dixie and my favorite color is gray. The Confederate flag represents the thirteen southern states that I love. My hero is general Robert E. Lee, and if I can ever get any money I intend to erect a statue of him in my yard underneath my high flying Confederate flag. Of course right away I'll be accused of being a racist which I'm certainly not. It's so easy to have the race card played against you. Just for example, the movie actor, Robert De Niro, has been married to a black woman for most of his adult life and he'll accuse me for being a racist because I chose to marry a white woman. He's played a tough guy in movie scripts for so long he actually thinks that he's bad. The last time I saw him on television he looked like an old worn out man and would fit the mold of being a pussy rather then a tough guy.

Has beens like Flo Rectum, of the television show the view is a good example of being in the classification of a moron. She looks to me as being a washed up jerk that has failed in everything she ever tried. She's nothing but a closed minded bitch that cries all the time about Hillary losing the presidential race to President Trump. Actually everyone on their show are flaming ass liberals that amount to nothing more than being play objects for horney men. Well, maybe not for Whoopie Goldberg. I can't imagine any man that would possibly be that horney and drunk to be attracted to her. I don't think Flo Rectum, would have to worry too much about men chasing her either with a face like hers.

I love America, but there's still a part of my heart and soul that still belongs to the old south. I've always wanted a civil war cannon or at least a replica to place in my yard next to my flag. Wishing for the cannon seemed hopeless and you know what they say about that, wish in one hand and shit in the other and see which one gets filled up first. I'd be happy to be able to buy a replica cannon if I could find one. I have looked everywhere and had no luck at all finding someone that builds them. It sure would look nice sitting out there in my yard with a stack of cannon balls next to it.

Years ago when I was still healthy and able to get around I drove out west to see the rest of our country and missed going to Mount Rushmore which I've regretted ever since. I've always thought that President Ronald Reagan's image should have been engraved on Mount Rushmore with the others. President Reagan, saved our country from Jimmy Carter and President Trump, is trying his best to save our country from the Democratic Party and eight years of the Obama administration. Now that I look at it, both of them Reagan and Trump belong on Mount Rushmore. It could easily be done by private donations and it's a shame that someone with influence hasn't started a campaign to do it.

Just like the wall that we need on our southern border. That wall could be constructed by private donations and be just like the wall in Israel. As far as I'm concerned it should be solid concrete and at least forty feet high. This man called Trump came just in time to save America and the most important attribute is the fact that he's not a lawyer. Rest assured, future generations will read about him and realize that he saved our country from the forces of evil. I think of him as Donald "backbone" Trump and the days of America being pushed around and taken advantage of are over. The open doors of our country are being shut to stop the illegal tide of immigrants from pouring in and signing up for welfare. Half of the people in the united states don't even pay any income taxes and they live off the earnings and taxes that the other half pays. Someday the half that works will wake up and realize that it doesn't pay to work will decide to sit on their ass too. With everyone sitting on their ass expecting the government to provide for them, how long do you think that our country can survive? It's almost getting to that point now and yet illegal immigrants are still climbing the border fence to get into the land of milk and honey. If President Trump can fulfill all his campaign promises his image will belong on Mount Rushmore for sure.

Sometimes I sit on my porch and think about my problems which seem overwhelming at times. I know that when I die, nothing will change. The earth will keep turning and no one outside of my immediate family will never know that I even existed and better yet they couldn't care less. Ask yourself if you ever accomplished anything worthwhile in your lifetime and did it make a difference for the good in someone else's life? For me personally I don't feel that anyone will remember me for too long because I never was the kind of person to impress other people. I think my immediate family might remember me for a few days depending on when they run out of money. When all the bills start pouring in at the end of the month they will probably remember me. I'm sure all the ones that I owe money to will keep me in mind. I only wish that I can live long enough to see all the lawyers, judges and trailer trash stand good for what they've done to me. I only wish that I was still in good health so I could see the look on their face when they turn around one day and I'm standing there in their presence for payment of their debt. Just because someone wears a coat and tie doesn't make that person an honorable person. On the contrary now days it's proper attire for crooks to wear while they're robbing someone as in my case. Dealing with well dressed thieves that usually hold a license to steal is worse then being robbed at gun point by some scumbag on the street. Dealing with them reminds me to send in a donation to PETA, people for the ethical treatment of animals. I do so because I love animals more than most human beings, especially those that are known as officers of the court. Every time I see an advertisement for a "pro bass shop" I send in another donation to PETA. I love animals and it does my heart good to see a big beautiful deer come into my yard and curious raccoons coming upon my porch. The animal world is a beautiful world and it bothers me greatly to see the human world doing everything it can do to destroy it. The pro bass shops take great pride in selling all kinds of hunting equipment to kill animals. It bothers the hell out of me to see some great white hunter put out a pile of sweet corn to attract some poor hungry deer then sit in a blind or climb a tree and wait for the deer so he can blow the poor animals head off as he feeds on the corn with a high powered rifle. They think that it's even more fun and sport if they can hit the poor animal with a steel tipped arrow. There are actually companies that place animals on certain areas of property just for the purpose of letting hunters come onto the land, hunt down the animals and slaughter them for sport. People that have this kind of mentality should be committed into a mental institution because they're mentally unstable. If they think that it's such a great and exciting sport then why don't they hide in the woods and let other hunters hunt them down and shoot their ass? As for me I'll take an animal anyday over some dumbass human being.

When I see forest fires burning down thousands of acres of forest, houses and trees, my main concern is for all the animals and foul it bothers me that thousands of God's little creatures are being killed. My heart bleeds for all the poor animals being forced out of their natural habitat by the expansion of cities. It seems like human beings won't be satisfied until they completely destroy everything that is good and beautiful about our planet including the oceans. After they have destroyed everything beautiful about our planet they'll destroy themselves. They tell me that animals have no soul and if that's true then God's work had one big flaw. I know that animals can hurt and feel pain just like any other creature on earth including humans. An animal can sense the difference between love and hate. A trait that most humans don't possess. Even a household pet knows right from wrong which is another trait that most humans disregard if it interferes in the slightest with their life. If someone comes to my house the last thing they should ever do is be mean or abuse one of my pets. My welcome mat is displayed for animals and family at my house and no one else until proven otherwise. It seems like disappointments come by quite regularly in my life.

Take the case of the Republican Party and especially the case of Senator John McCain. He makes a very moving speech before the senate saying how everyone should stick together to get things accomplished. Two days later he turns around and votes no on a bill to advance the effort to repeal and replace the disaster known as Obamacare. He stabbed the Republican Party in the back along with the senator from Alaska, Markowski and the senator from Maine, Collins. These three senators killed any effort by the Republican Party to repeal Obamacare. Hopefully, these three so-called republicans will get voted out of office in the next election before they can do anymore damage to the party. Considering how screwed up our country is the only thing that will wake America up is for the little fat "rocket man" in North Korea to drop a bomb on Los Angeles, California. All the freeloaders and protesters will be so busy looking for a place to hide to save their ass they won't be concerned with trying to get more free stuff from the government. One thing for sure we won't be able to depend on all of the little chicken shits that spend all of their time protesting and destroying property to fight for our country in time of need.

Every now and then I just get damn tired of being white. Hell, I'm blamed for everything from causing people to have hemorrhoids to slavery. I'm blamed for screwing blacks out of jobs and who knows what else. I think I'd like to be black for awhile and get on the gravy train of so-called oppression. I could discriminate against some of the pain in the ass whites and get their jobs with the help of affirmative action and enjoy the feeling of screwing someone else for a change. I've always heard that once you're black you'll never go back. I'd like to know what it feels like to be chased by a lot of white women that are known as groupies. I can only imagine what a fun night it would be on a Saturday night drunk on my ass, dancing with all the drunk ass ladies down at Jesse Red's Lounge. I wouldn't have to worry about trying to pass the promotional exam on the department. My color and affirmative action would take care of any problems I might have with the department. I would have to give plenty of thought to getting a promotion or job because I would lose too much in the way of benefits. It seems like the system created by white honkies encourages me to stay where I'm at and be happy. They may kick me out of my federal housing apartment and cut off my supply of food stamps, but I couldn't careless because there's more than one way to skin a cat. Cutting some of my benefits don't scare me in the least. They can do whatever they please but I'd much rather be black then a white cracker. If I ever get tired of being black which I seriously doubt then maybe I'd go for being brown.

Being classified as a Mexican, I'd have the world by the balls so to speak. As soon as I enter the U.S.A. I'd automatically qualify for welfare benefits such as food stamps, housing, jobs and medical care for my baby which is due at any time. It's obvious that if you're a condom salesman in Mexico you'll starve to death. The idea for the Mexican women is to get knocked up in Mexico and come to the united states to give birth to their new baby and that way it will be a citizen of the states. That way if the U.S. authorities start to deport the mother for being an illegal immigrant she will scream bloody murder that you're splitting up the family. She's right, send the kids back with her where they all belong.

On second thought maybe I'd rather be brown than black, but one thing for sure not white. I have even considered being yellow, but knowing how liberals think they'd probably blame me for bombing Pearl Harbor. At least being white as I am now the assholes can't blame me for Pearl Harbor. Have you noticed how every time there's a disturbance or riot it was caused by a white supremacist or white nationalist people according to the liberal left. Maybe I'm wrong but it certainly seems that ignorant and stupid people are favored and showered with welfare benefits not offered to the working class. It reminds me of what Benjamin Franklin once said, "We all are born ignorant, but one must work hard to remain stupid". If I had ever dreamed that ignorance would be so rewarded and overlooked I would never have worked my ass off to get educated. I have a wall full of college degrees and certificates of recognition for accomplishments for what they're worth which is nothing. Under the present circumstances they'd make better toilet paper then credentials for obtaining a good job as a result of affirmative action. That fact will remain until the morons in every level of government accepts the real fact that affirmative action has long outlived it's usefulness and does nothing now but falsely discriminate against people. How many more generations does the government think that affirmative action needs to apply? They said that it was necessary to level the playing field which has turned out to be a joke. The National Football League is 75% black and the national basketball league is almost 100% black. Whatever happened to that level playing field? I've learned in my life that when you give something to someone try and take it back. Professional sports pays millions of dollars to the players and it just reminds me of what Benjamin Franklin, said about being born ignorant and becoming stupid.

When I was a police officer I was hammered down by the system until I had to retire in the hope that I could live as an equal citizen and rid myself of the bleeding hearts and ass kissers that saturated the department. As in the city of Miami police department, the Dade County Sheriff's Office slowly evolved from an ass kicking department to an ass kissing department. One day you may be heading a specialized unit and the next day you may find yourself working under the supervision of someone that didn't display the intelligence of a seventh grader in junior high school I have never understood the justification of paying chief executive officers of businesses, county managers and yes politicians such outrageously high salaries for making a decision which had been discussed by a dozen other people for the previous six months. Can you imagine getting paid millions of dollars for basically sitting on your ass in some office and finalizing a decision. When a CEO is finally run off he is given thousands of shares of the company stock and millions in severance pay. He walks out rich as hell and the poor stock holders get screwed again. The jerk CEO usually goes to another company and it starts all over again.

Talk about how people get mistreated and screwed look to the American Indians. Boy, did the white man ever give them a good screwing. In retrospect they were probably the most mistreated people on earth and our government should be completely ashamed of itself. I personally admire Crazy Horse and Geronimo for their resistance of being slaughtered and placed on reservations. In a way I'm glad that General George Custer got his ass shot off at the Little Big Horn. He was there for no other reason then rounding up the Indians and driving them to a reservation. Well, the Seventh Calvary lost that battle and you can say they died with their boots on. God bless the American Indians.

Our country is so divided now I don't see how it can possibly recover and become united again. It's certainly not the country that I grew up in. We have people like George Soros who has more money then brains supporting and funding every radical movement that he can find. In my opinion the movement to destroy southern heritage by removing Confederate statues was started and encouraged by the ex-governor of South Carolina, Nikki Haley, when she ordered the Confederate flag removed from Columbia. Now you have every knee jerk politician thinking if they do the same it will get them votes when they run for re-election. They cave in to the racist and organizations like antifa because they're too scared to do otherwise. Getting votes and staying in office is more important then what is right or wrong. The morons can remove every Confederate statue in the country and it still doesn't change anything. The governor of Virginia has shown that he too has his head up his ass too like all the rest of the southern haters. For all the politicians and everyone else that supports removing Confederate statues and flags, I want all of them to know that they're more then welcome to kiss my rebel ass. Not on the right side or the left side but dead center in the middle.

I was born and raised in the south by the grace of God and if anyone doesn't like it they can go straight to hell and the sooner the better. I have a Confederate flag flying on my property and I will shoot any son of a bitch that tries to take it down. I was never raised to hate anyone but it seems that there are forces within our society determined that I take sides in order to defend my right to exist and birth right. That's one of the main reasons I'm just damn tired of being white and getting blamed for everything. To make things worse we're flooded with college students that don't know their ass from a hole in the ground about anything. Most graduate with an I.Q. level of an idiot because they were taught by professors that spent most of their time bashing and cursing America and what she stands for. A large majority of students went to college just to party and get drunk on their ass. Paying the tuition didn't bother them at all if mommy and daddy didn't pay it. They'd just float a government loan and worry about it later. Some students apparently majored in rioting 101 and just being plain stupid. Ask the average college student what are the three branches of government and they have no idea what you're talking about. Right now there is a movement to destroy the country's history and remove anything that relates to the old south. We can thank Governor Nikki Haley, for creating that radical movement. In my opinion it's getting high time for our country to experience another revolution to re-establish the foundation that made America great in the first place. And to rid ourselves of thugs that protest the right of other people to assemble and express their views whether it's the black panther party or the Ku Klux Klan. No thugs or protesters have the right to deny a person his or her freedom of speech. President Trump was elected President and the communist fringe, liberals and brain dead college students need to get over it. They represent the worse of society and are constantly showing their ignorance.

The best and sure way of restoring America and what she used to stand for would be to suspend the U.S. Constitution for ten years and show the people what it means to obey the law and the right of the people to peacefully assemble without being interfered with.

If this can't be done then it's high time for the citizens to arm themselves and use those arms whenever necessary to insure their right of free speech. At the incident in Charlottesville, Virginia, the police chief either didn't know what to do regarding potential trouble or was completely incompetent and should be replaced for dereliction of duty. A lot of people are appointed to high positions of authority that have no idea what they're doing or how to manage the position. I speak from actual experience of seeing it occur in a large police department myself. Most command positions in police departments are filled by the authority of close friends and rarely have anything to do with knowledge and ability. I've seen officers with years of experience and college degrees passed over for promotion due to nothing more then the color of their skin. I'm convinced that some people just can't make a decision when a situation confronts them. I will relate an incident that occurred to me when I was an officer on the Dade County Sheriff's Office. I came on duty one night and immediately responded to an incident where a pizza delivery man was stabbed by a customer. When I arrived at the scene I observed numerous officers standing around in the front yard of a house talking to the on duty staff officer. I asked the staff officer to fill me in on what had occurred and he told me that the individual in the house had ordered a pizza and when he opened the front door to take the pizza from the delivery man, he stabbed the man in the stomach with a large knife for no apparent reason. I asked the staff duty officer why hasn't the subject been arrested and he responded that he had sent one officer downtown to obtain an arrest warrant from a judge. Can you believe that bullshit? The staff duty officer has the rank of police captain and doesn't know his ass from a hole in the ground. I went to the front door and observed the subject washing the knife off at the kitchen sink. With the help of another officer we kicked the door open arrested the subject and impounded the knife for evidence. When I cleared the scene the staff duty officer was still standing there waiting for the unneeded warrant. He was a prime example of someone that didn't know how to do his job. He would have served himself much better in life if he was a vacuum cleaner salesman or selling shoes at sears. Some people have a born personality to lead and it comes naturally. Some supervisors like this particular staff duty officer don't have the ability to be a Boy Scout leader.

A simple rule when enforcing the law is, was there a law violated and is this the person that violated that law? If it is then arrest him or her and throw their ass into jail. I never hesitated to arrest anyone that needed to be arrested and anyone that decided to resist arrest got his ass kicked if it became necessary. Getting my ass kicked was not in the job description and nor was I hired to be anyones punching bag. I never hesitated to play Dixie on some punk's head with my flashlight or night stick if he chose to fight. As a supervisor if an officer brought a subject into the station under arrest with a completed use of force form then I wanted to see the prisoner with a fat lip or a knot on his head. On one occasion I had a young police officer bring a prisoner into the station which he had also charged with resisting arrest. The officer had his own shirt torn half off, skinned up and looked like he had been dragged through the mud. The subject didn't have one mark on him and appeared to be quite alright except for his big mouth. Needless to say I spent the next hour in my office with the young officer explaining to him that it's not expected of him to get assaulted and beat up by anyone. In the future if anyone assaults you, make that person pay a price before it becomes a habit with him. It's called adjusting their attitude which becomes necessary every now and then.

It's hard for the average citizen that has never been in law enforcement to understand the concept of roadside justice. I always tried to play by the rules and ignore being called unpleasant names. It wasn't unusual to have my family tree traced but occasionally all the rules would go out the window and not exist the second some wise ass punk sucker punches you in the mouth. That's when I would immediately subject him to some good old fashion roadside justice and take great pleasure in doing so. If you assault me then rest assured I will do my very best to unscrew your head. Sometimes things happened that really bothered my soul. I was dispatched to a bar fight at the lighthouse bar and ended up having to arrest a good friend of mine from high school. I was one of those police officers that applied the law equally to everyone and considered giving someone a break was a professional weakness which I didn't have at that time.

At the present our country is in need of change big time. I see big mouth female protesters that act and talk like common sluts. Their heroes are washed up women like muff diver Posie O'Ronald, Pewdonna, Bathy Sniffin and Ashely Mudd. All of them are has beens that reek with stupidity. Colleges have gone to hell and have taken most of the students with them. A lot of the freeloading students major in rioting 101 because they don't have brains enough to excel in anything else. The communist movement in America is alive and well. The black female that climbed up to the Confederate statue to tie a rope around it in Durham, North Carolina so the other nit wits on the ground could pull it down is an active member of a front for the communist party. The half wits on the ground protesting and spitting on the fallen statue are nothing but ignorant freeloading trash. Their brain reminds me of having a b-b in a thimble. A lot of them attend college at daddy and mommy's expense because they're too damn lazy to work. They're basically in college to get drunk, smoke pot and get laid which doesn't appear on many job applications for work. After graduation they're not even qualified to flip hamburgers at McDonald's much less enter the cooperate world of business. They can always make some extra money by being paid to protest at some conservative rally or speaking engagement. They'll carry around some half wit goofy sign as they shoot their filthy mouths off for an hour or so and they consider it all in a days work. Most of them are so stupid they have no idea what it's all about. They have to be careful because someday enough of the good people will get tired of it and a backlash will occur putting an end to it and them. There seems to be no end to their gross ignorance and the day will come that the monster they have created will destroy them in the name of goodness and mercy. Nothing ever stays the same and everything on earth is in a constant state of change and that includes human behavior. Take the imbeciles at Durham, North Carolina that tore down the statue of the Confederate soldier. They are nothing but empty headed morons that know absolutely nothing about the civil war. They are totally ignorant of history and most of the college students no doubt major in sex, drugs and how to get laid and cheat.

For the black jerk that tied the rope around the statue of the Confederate soldier, she should be thanking the old south for slavery otherwise she'd probably be in Africa running around with a spear chasing something to eat and living in squalor. Destroying Confederate statues doesn't have a thing to do with racism, it's a political movement by the democratic left and where does it stop? Are the idiots going to go and destroy the Thomas Jefferson Memorial because after all he was a slave owner even if he did write most of our constitution. That document was written and composed by old white men that also owned slaves. While they're at it maybe they'd like to destroy every statue of George Washington too and tear up the U.S. constitution. Like I've said before ignorance knows no boundaries and right now we have nothing but wall to wall ignorance. We have one brain dead council woman in Baltimore comparing general Robert E. Lee to Adolph Hitler. Talk about complete ignorance if that dumbass had any brains she'd really be dangerous.

Those little ball-less wonders had the Confederate statues removed from public property by city workers at night. I wonder how many statues of the known jail bird Martin Luther King are on public property? Today we have the idiots destroying our history and wearing their racism as a badge of honor. Tomorrow maybe it will be book burning as the Nazis did in Germany. I congratulate and commend Sheriff Mike Andrews of Durham, North Carolina for enforcing the law against people destroying property. That was refreshing after seeing how the police in Charlottesville, Virginia did nothing. It would appear that the chief of police in in Durham sided with the protesters and had his officers show up with riot gear and do nothing to restore order. Either he supported the rioters or didn't know what the hell to do. I have personally participated in riots as a police officer and to see officers doing nothing to prevent and stop a riot is total incompetence and the Durham police chief should be replaced and find a job at McDonald's where he will fit in and feel more comfortable.

The blacks including that dumbass black council woman in Baltimore that compared general Robert E. Lee to Adolph Hitler had better be thankful that Hitler lost the war. If Hitler had won the war you can only imagine what he had in store for the black race. As much as he hated the Jewish people it couldn't possibly compare what he had planned for the black race if he won the war. The war cost America the lives of 425,000 servicemen of which I may add thousands were southern white men. The country is plagued by gangs of nit wits that represents nothing in life vandalizing and destroying Confederate monuments. They are mostly illiterate trash completely ignorant of the war between the states. I don't believe that most of them even knew about the civil war much less know anything about it. They recently vandalized the Lincoln Memorial and of course nothing will be done about it as usual. Let's see if the gutless chicken shit wonders destroy the statues of George Washington and the Thomas Jefferson Memorial too. It's high time for the people to rise up in our country and put a stop to all the rampant lawlessness. The only thing that lawless thugs understand is brute force delivered in a way that will get the immediate attention of worthless trash offenders. You really don't have to be too concerned regarding the loss of life because humans breed like flies and the earth is overrun with the human population. There are even billion people on earth and that should tell you something. It has been suggested in the past that babies should be neutered at birth because that's the only way that the population can be controlled. Living in squalor means nothing to millions of people and their basic form of entertainment is screwing each others brains out. Squirting out babies is no more important then drinking a Coke and eating a Moon Pie. Most people are wise to the system and squirt out more babies in order to get more welfare. Millions of people south of our southern border pour into our country seeking a free ride at tax payer's expense and they get it.

I drive a twenty one year old junk vehicle that's in the shop again right now having more work done on it because I can't afford to buy anything and yet I see Mexicans and other south Americans who are probably illegal driving around in brand new vehicles which really frost my balls.

Regarding terrorism, anytime a person is caught doing an act of terrorism they should be executed, their entire family deported and their house bulldozed to the ground. For a U.S. citizen caught destroying property public or private and convicted should be incarcerated for a mandatory ten years and fined twenty five thousand dollars. Enough is enough and the miscarriages of the human race should feel the wrath of wrong doing in a way that they won't forget. Anyone found guilty of vandalism should have their sorry ass caned in the public square for everyone to watch. One thing that would straighten up America for sure is if that little fat rocket man in North Korea dropped a bomb on us. People would be so busy trying to find a place to hide their ass all of the knee down and bitching about racism shit would be forgotten. They'd stop bitching about the government and be begging for the government to save their sorry ass. To hell with all the statues and other chicken shit silly non sense, just save my ass. When the going gets tough you'll see the overpaid NFL football players get off their knees and run like hell.

President Trump should have run as an independent and let the Republican Party establishment stay in the swamp with the democrats where they belong. Too many republicans are in name only and should belong to the Democratic Party with Chuck Schumer and Nancy Greaserack. So-called republicans like John McCain, Merkowski, Collins and many others should be voted out of office and the Republican Party. They are part of the Washington swamp that needs to be drained. I don't know what Senator Lindsley Grahm of South Carolina has been smoking but he needs to keep his mouth shut and stop encouraging the nit wits to destroy Confederate monuments and criticizing President Trump. If you can't support him then leave the party and join your liberal friends. I appreciate the fact that

Senator Grahm did vote recently for the tax reform bill and supported President Trump.

If people think that we'll never see another terrible thing that happened in Nazi Germany when millions of innocent people were exterminated, you had better think again. History always repeats itself and someday down the road the world will witness the destruction of a people beyond belief and there's nothing capable of preventing it. It will happen as surely as the sun will rise tomorrow morning. When it occurs I'll be resting in my grave with no problems or worries. It's amazing how a person's mind can drift back into time and remember something during times of unrest and turmoil. I remember how my dear mother would sit at her old piano and sing a song as she played a beautiful song named "beautiful redwing." as mom sang my dad would be sitting in his favorite chair as I shined his shoes and he would always ask me "son, do you think you'll ever amount to anything?" those are the good memories that I will take to my grave.

When you get old and living the twilight years of your life you don't need a doctor to tell you when you're going to die, nature will tell you so save your money. The future won't mean that much to you and you will always find yourself drifting back into your past. For instance your first love and the experience of being so deeply in love with another person. I will never forget my undying love for my first love and how it affected my young life. She was a majorette in the marching band at Miami Jackson High School and I carried her picture in my billfold for sixty years never to see or hear from her again. Her name was Gail Ackerman and she was my beautiful angel. She moved to Galveston, Texas because her father lost his job at the Miami Herald and had to move to Galveston for another job. Every time Gail wrote to me she would always write SWAK on the back of the envelope which stood for "sealed with a kiss." She would always tell me that it was "sealed with a kiss and if you love me you'll always remember this." One time and a million years later so it seemed I thought I had located her on the internet but never got to talk to her before she disappeared again. I drove my old 1941 Ford Coupe with twelve pounds of oil pressure all the way to Galveston, Texas to see her. I was only seventeen years old and going that far away by myself driving such an old car must have worried my poor mother to death. When I got there we went out to the movies and saw "The Prisoner of Zenda" with James Mason. After the movie we went and parked on top of the seawall and talked about all the good times that we had together in Miami before she had to move to Texas. She was wearing a white sweater and looked as beautiful as ever. That night when I picked her up at her house there was some young fellow at her house which I know now was someone that she was seeing. He was at her house no doubt to see what I looked like. When we were apart I wrote her everyday during my sixth period class in high school. Gail must be close to eighty years of age by now and I'll bet ten dollars to a donut that she is beautiful as ever. I've often wondered if she still lives at 1218 Bayou Shore Drive in Galveston. Every time I heard the singer Glen Campbell sing the song "Galveston" I always thought of Gail. At that time in my young life God made nothing stronger than the love I had for Gail. Welcome to a thing called "jury nullification" in which jurors are encouraged to vote not guilty regardless of the evidence. Hang the jury and to hell with justice.

It has gotten to the point in my life that I can't understand most people. They object and protest to almost everything until it has become a way of life for them. In Asheville, North Carolina we have our share of weirdos that spend most of their time just loitering around downtown and doing nothing. Then we have those people that will always show up carrying their signs protesting something. We call them "cave people", citizens against virtually everything. Then occasionally we will have the ladies congregate in front of the police station exposing their tattooed and sagging tits for everyone to see including the police. The police never take any action and just stand around gawking at them. They certainly aren't good looking women and some have tits that hang so low they look like a couple of huge nuts. It's rumored that the female police chief is a bonafide muff diver herself and I suppose that's why the police don't do anything but gawk. This is a good example of people needing their sorry ass kicked good. It wouldn't surprise me in the least if Nancy Greaserack didn't show up at one of their gatherings because she's such a strong supporter of women's rights. Years ago before she got old and worn out looking she was voted "miss grease rack" in some contest. I'll bet she's had her rack greased quite a few times over the years. I have no proof but I personally think that she's a closet drunk. I base my suspicion on the fact that I've arrested hundreds of drunks during my career in law enforcement. She's just another democrat that can't accept the fact that crooked Hillary lost the election again. Hillary is still in a state of shock. Look at the way she pranced around with a big grin waving to everyone thinking that she had the election in the bag and she was going to be the President of the United States. Oh, she was so happy and even had the oval office measured for new drapes. She ordered a truck load of fireworks for the big celebration. It just didn't happen and to lose for the second time was too much for her to accept. She just had a book published about the presidential race entitled "what happened." her and her husband slick willy, made a fortune and became multi-millionaires with their so-called Clinton foundation. When Bill Clinton was President he was apparently starved for sexual attention to the point that he had to resort to getting blowjobs in the oval office by a twenty year old intern. I'll bet that was one fine tasting cigar that the President kept sticking into his mouth and sucking on. Hillary was nasty as hell to all of the secret service officers and was just downright hateful to them. Some people suggested that maybe she was going through menopause and with Bill's extra activity in the oval office it affected her about everything. The poor secret service officers couldn't do anything right according to Hillary and apparently neither could Bill.

Well enough said about their sexual problems. Hillary could have solved all those problems if she made those trips to the islands with Bill and his special friend. When Hillary and Bill die they'll have to screw both of them into the ground because both of them have been crooked for so long they'll never fit them into a casket. The best things in life are free so they say and neither of them had to devote their lives stealing whatever they could. Of course I understand that both of them attended law school and that explains why they had an uncontrolled desire to steal from other people. It's such a trait with lawyers I wouldn't be surprised if there was a required course designated stealing 101.

Then we have the NFL football players who are nothing but overpaid entertainers sitting on their ass and kneeling to disrespect our national anthem and flag. By doing so they disrespect the 425,000 soldiers that were killed in world war two, who gave their lives fighting for their freedom. I realize now that they would be better suited for hanging on the back of a garbage truck picking up garbage. These idiots only magnify the ignorance that so many of their kind display in their culture. Why the NFL owners pay these jerks so much money to play a game that requires so little brains is beyond me. They are paid millions of dollars and two years after leaving the NFL you'll find them working at burger king or McDonald's because they'll be broke as hell. The smart ones will invest their money for their future but some will turn to unsavory occupations like pimping. Most pimps can be easily recognized by the large gold chains hanging around their necks and driving large expensive cars.

The democrats on the left, young morons and ignorant college students that assault people trying to have a peaceful gathering had better wake up if possible which I personally doubt. They protest everything and don't even know what they're protesting about. Most are brainless nit wits that can't even figure out what is the sum total of two plus two. A large part of them live on welfare and still sponge off mommy and daddy at home. Between them and the lame brain assholes that call themselves antifa they are creating a Frankenstein monster that will raise up and destroy them. One day they may well be standing on the edge of a pit facing a firing squad that sends them to hell where they belong. They think they can bash southern whites, the police and our country's history for as long as they please because they're so ignorant, but one day the end will come. Pay back is going to be a bitch conducted in a wild frenzy like the world has never seen. Hitler's holocaust will seem like a picnic when it begins and there won't be anyplace to hide. The anti-America people will pay the price and nothing will be able to stop it because it will be supported by millions of people that were pushed to the breaking point and simply had enough. Like I've said before the only way to get America back on track is to suspend the U.S. constitution for ten years. No one should be entitled to the protection of the constitution until the constitution is reinstated. Neutralize lawyers in their constant pursuit to sue people over the slightest thing in order to rob them. Lawyers robbing people would be a thing of the past as well as "turn em lose" judges that are nothing more then a hemorrhoid to society. Think about it. There's nothing that you can't be sued for in our society. If someone farts on a crowded elevator you had better hope there's no lawyer on the elevator because if there is you can expect a lawsuit coming down the pike and everyone on the elevator can expect a subpoena to give depositions to testify against the guilty party. The lawyer will probably issue subpoenas for people at the environmental protection agency to appear in court to testify about the quality of air in the elevator when the defendant farted. Knowing how the courts operate and the awards handed out each person on the elevator would probably receive 15 to 20 thousand dollars apiece. This is just an example of how our court system operates today and the bullshit that a lawyer will stoop to for money.

Regarding Afghanistan if I was running things there would be only two options facing that country. I would either make the entire country a parking lot or I'd get the hell out. America has been fighting their war for the past sixteen years at the cost of trillions of dollars and the lives of twenty five hundred American soldiers. The loss of one American Marine means more to me then all of the camel jockeys in Afghanistan. Apparently the Russians have more brains then Americans when it comes to fighting a worthless war. They were fighting in Afghanistan for eight years and recognized that it just wasn't worth it and pulled out. Then of all things the united states went over and took their place. America seems to have a record of sticking it's nose into every problem on the planet. George Washington, told us not to involve ourselves in foreign affairs and we never took his advice. One good example is how we lost the lives of 55,000 American soldiers in Vietnam and please tell me what the hell was accomplished? We've already restored diplomatic relations with Vietnam and realize that we got our ass kicked by a rag tag army. I could never understand why we would send our soldiers into the jungle looking for the enemy. Exposing them to gunfire and getting them killed was a dumbass way of fighting a war. America should have made parking lots out of their cities so they wouldn't have anything to fight for or homes to go back to. You have to destroy a man's will to fight and having nothing to go back to is the best way of doing it.

Guerilla warfare is the way the south should have fought the civil war between the states. Tradition called for each side to meet in a large open area, line up facing each other and start shooting each other. No wonder 750,000 lives were lost in that war. My name is also Robert E. Lee, but I would never have engaged a battle doing something stupid like that. The north fought battles the same way and both sides had a lot to learn. In Vietnam they used guerilla tactics and their rag tag army kicked America's ass. Of course the usual protesters running up and down Pennsylvania Avenue in front of the White House didn't help and only encouraged the Vietcong to keep on fighting.

Nothing surprises me anymore. Recently a judge in Ohio was ambushed and shot on his way to the courthouse. Considering some of the biased rulings that I've seen judges make robbing the hell out of some poor slob it's a wonder that more judges haven't been shot. Between the lawyers and judges it's a wonder there's not an open season on both of them.

This is how outrageous lawsuits have become. Some woman developed a cancer of the vagina and immediately thought of a way to sue a company for causing it. She finds a lawyer and they plan their course of action. The lawyer took a page right out of Jesse Fraction's play book on how to get rich suing large corporations. The woman tells the lawyer that for years she had sprinkled Johnson's baby powder on her crotch and the crotch of her panties and it caused her ovarian cancer. As absurd as it sounds the court awarded her 417 million dollars. She has opened the door for all the men that has developed throat cancer as a result of having oral sex with her. It's a known medical fact that sucking on a woman's vagina can give a person throat cancer. So all you muff divers be aware that your sore throat could be cancer. Don't laugh about the Johnson's baby powder because I've thought about sprinkling it on my ass and having a lawyer claim that it gave me a bad case of hemorrhoids. Hell, I could make millions but knowing my luck I wouldn't be awarded $4.00 and I'd owe the snake lawyer $3,000.00 for filing the case. Even turning out bad for me I'm sure I would have had a truck load of lawyers wanting to take such a worthwhile case. As far as the baby powder on a muff I certainly wouldn't appreciate coming up and having my face covered with baby powder.

Sort of stupid isn't it but that's how far out our court system has become and it's only the tip of the iceberg. Awarding someone 417 million dollars as a result of having an itchy crotch is insane and there must be a limit set for paying a settlement. Can't you just imagine how much the lawyer is going to take out of such large settlements. No wonder law schools are filled up with crooks. After the lawyer takes his cut no doubt he'll have to pay the judge for rendering such a ridiculous settlement. Pulling a trick like that a few times, the lawyer and his friend the judge will retire super rich. For money like that you can cover my ass with Johnson's baby powder, sprinkle it on my head and I'll even snort the shit for you.

The country that I grew up in doesn't exist anymore. All of the idiots doing the protesting appear to be young people that don't know their ass from a hole in the ground and no doubt live on welfare and are still sponging off mommy and daddy. They represent nothing but anarchy and will hire out to anyone as a protester. They remind me of the movie "Walking Dead" and that's a compliment. The female protesters appear to be real loose and their only real reason for being with the crowd is to serve as cum receptacles between protest for the scumbag males. Just looking at the females I think I'd much rather make love to Mrs. Palm and her five daughters rather then contract some sexually transmitted disease from one of the douchebag protesters. Anytime there is violence and destruction of property I'm all in favor of using lethal and deadly force. It's time for strong action to be taken against the scum because that's all they understand. The radical left of the Democratic Party, political correctness and America hating thugs and scumbags have done everything they can to destroy America and what it stands for. I knew the country was going to hell when I saw an empty suit like Obama get elected twice as President. Then we had former President George Bush, just sitting on his ass and refusing to criticize Obama for anything. When asked why he doesn't have anything to say, he said that it's not nice for a former President to criticize a sitting President. A simple explanation is that he didn't have any balls. He obviously talks out of both sides of his mouth because just recently he stood on a world stage and bashed President Trump's policies. I wonder what happened to it wouldn't be nice? Then of all things his own elderly father told the world that President Trump is a blowhard. The entire Bush family remains pissed because brother Jeb lost to Donald Trump in the nomination process and they can't get over it. One thing for sure and hopefully all the parties can accept it. The Clintons and Bush family are finished for good so get over it and find something else to do with your lives.

I voted for Trump for a few good reasons. He wasn't a damn lawyer which gave him a truck load of credibility. He promised to build a wall on our southern border with Mexico and address the illegal immigration problem. Right now the democrats in the senate are doing everything they can to stop any money from going to build the wall. I personally think that the wall should be one like Israel has and at least 40 feet high. The best and sure way of getting enough money for the wall is through private donations. If everyone that voted for Trump would send in one hundred dollars we'd have enough money to build two or three walls.

President Trump should start a nationwide campaign for donations and screw the democrats. That way he wouldn't have to give up anything he wants to do to please and bargain with the democrats. No wall should be built that you can see through because if you can see them they can sure as hell see you. It would be best that they not know what we're doing on our side. The wall should be poured concrete and steel and at least 4 or 5 feet thick and extend into the ground at least 8 feet with sound sensors.

The Republican Party people had better wake up, stand up and be counted before we lose our country to scumbag protesters like antifa and brain dead misguided assholes like you see demonstrating against everything we love. Stop dreaming about owning that new car, living in a fancy new home and living the good life while our country and world is crumbling down around you. I'm nothing but a crippled old man 83 years old that has the heart of a young man with an undying love for our country and a drive to save our country from the thieves that are doing everything possible to destroy our way of life and our heritage. One of the primary reasons that it's happening to our country is because of illegal immigrants pouring into our country unchecked. If I was only a young man and with God given strength I'd lead a crusade against the evil forces that are tearing our beloved country apart. As I've said before President Trump should tell the democrats in congress that refuse to appropriate money for the border wall to go to hell. In my opinion hell is where most of them belong because most of them are nothing but self serving moron lawyers. We now have at least 800,000 people that were brought into our country by their parents when they were kids. All of them the parents and kids came into our country illegally and now the democrats want all of them to become citizens. Anyone that's standing in line to enter the United States and become a citizen should have their head examined because all you have to do now is simply walk in or get on top of a train boxcar and ride in.

I'm in favor of deporting everyone that's in our country illegally and that includes the kids too. Sending the kids back with them and we won't be guilty of breaking up the family. The nit wit ex-President Obama was the one that supported the so-called "DACA" program even after he said that he had no constitutional right to do it. Time has proven over and over that Obama was totally incompetent in domestic and foreign affairs. He was nothing but a community organizer in Chicago before becoming President. When President he hired racist like Eric Holder and Loretta Lynch, who fit his mold of thinking and between them they almost destroyed our country. All of the assholes aren't in congress because most of them are in television shows like the view. One of the biggest ones that I know of is Flo Rectum on the view. Talk about stupid she takes first prize besides being on the scary ugly side. When the movie industry was handing out awards to recognized actors they turned it into a Trump bashing show. I was really disappointed in Dolly Parton when she appeared on stage between two other Trump hating actors and stood there silent as they bashed Trump. I'm sorry Dolly, but you screwed up. It was your opportunity to show your grit and support for your country and President. You caved in rather then standing tall in front of a room full of assholes. The assholes standing next to you showed you no respect and placed you in an awkward position. I see Robert Deniro was there looking older then ever. I kept looking for my favorite actress Linda Lovelace, but she never showed up. She was in my favorite movie deep throat and probably had more talent then anyone in the building. I've learned that being beautiful doesn't necessarily make you smart. I look at the television show the view and being ugly must make a person stupid. Rachael Madcow has a television show where all she does is bash Trump and any republican. She's pretty and must have a train load of horney men chasing her around but although she's pretty, at times she seems to be on the dense side. There's one that scares the hell out of me when I see her on television. Her name is Frederica Wilson and she's a Florida representative. She wears ten gallon cowboy hats of many colors and large sunglasses. She's one ugly broad and now she thinks she's a rock star.

I feel sorry for the judge in Ohio that was shot going into the court-house and apparently he pissed off someone to a hateful degree like I was treated by the court system. As many bad decisions that judges make routinely it's a wonder that there's no open season on them. All of the lawyers and judges that I've had to deal with seem to believe that they can do whatever they please and to hell with the falsely ac-cused defendant that stands before them.

This is how outrageous lawsuits have become. Some woman devel-oped vagina cancer and right away thought of a way to sue some company for causing it. She dials up a lawyer and they plan their course of action. The lawyer takes a page right out of Jesse Fraction's play book on how to get rich suing large corporations. The wom-an tells the lawyer how she sprinkled Johnson's baby power on the crotch of her panties for years and on her muff and it caused her to have ovarian cancer. As absurd as it sounds the court awarded her 417 million dollars. The court has opened the door for all the men that has indulged in oral sex to make the claim that women gave them throat cancer and especially the women that sprinkled Johnston's baby powder on their muff. Now I see that some other woman has recently filed a lawsuit against some company because she has been sprinkling talcum powder on her muff and she developed cancer. In my opinion these lawsuits are nothing but a lot of bullshit. Can you imagine some lame brain judge awarding the complainant 417 million dollars for such an outrageous lawsuit? It makes me wonder why they wanted to put powder on their muff in the first place. As for me I certainly wouldn't appreciate coming up for air and having my face covered with baby or talcum powder. That's only an example of how the court system has gotten out of control and it's only the tip of the iceberg. Apparently the judge realized that the more money he awarded the complainant the more his kickback would be. For 417 million dollars you are welcome to cover my ass with Johnson's baby powder or talcum powder. Sprinkle it on top of my head and I'll even snort the shit for you. I'll put it in my coffee and cereal every morning for a lot less then 417 million dollars.

At present it's being shown that our federal government and the people in power during the Obama years are completely corrupt. I knew that the government was corrupt but I never dreamed that it involved the FBI director and even agents that worked for him. Their goal was to do whatever was necessary to protect Hillary and destroy President Trump. It's believed that even Obama has set up a shadow government to control when and where riots occur. Candidate Bernie Oddball was destroyed by the Clinton machine and if he had any common sense he'd team up with President Trump and help him drain the swamp and flush the sewer.

The country that I grew up in doesn't exist anymore. Brainless idiots protest everything and represent nothing but anarchy. What really surprised me was it seem to be represented by young people. The female protesters looked and acted like common trash. I suspect that their main purpose was to be cum receptacles for all the male protesters. Anytime there is destruction of property and businesses broken into I'm all in favor of using lethal and deadly force. It's time that for strong action be taken against the scum because that's all they understand. Most are no doubt living on welfare and have their pockets stuffed with food stamps that the tax payers are providing for them.

The Democratic Party, political correctness and the liberal left have done everything they can to destroy America and what it stands for. I knew the country was going to hell when an incompetent moron like Obama could get elected as President. Then we had a former President, George Bush, who just sat on his ass and refused to criticize Obama for anything he did because it wouldn't be nice for a former President to say anything bad about a sitting president. A simple explanation would be that he didn't have any balls.

I voted for President Trump for two reasons. He wasn't a lawyer and he promised to build a wall on our southern border with Mexico. The Democratic Party is doing everything possible to prevent the senate from appropriating the money for the construction of the wall. I personally feel that the wall should be like the one in Israel and at least forty feet high. The best and sure way of getting more than enough money to build the wall would be through private donations. President Trump should start a nationwide campaign for donations. If everyone that voted for Trump and anyone else that wants the wall would send in one hundred dollars he'd have enough money to build three walls and tell Chuck Schumer and Nancy Greaserack to go to hell no see through wall should be built because if you can see them they sure as hell can see if the border patrol is around some place. It's best that they are not able to see what is going on involving our security. In my opinion the wall should be 4 to 5 feet thick poured solid with concrete over a interior wall of steel rebars. If china can build a huge wall as wide as a roadway over 13,000 miles long over mountainous terrains solely by hand labor, don't tell me that we can't build a wall 1,700 miles long with modern machinery.

The people that love America had better stand up and wake up before we lose our country to the anarchist. Stop worrying about getting that nice new car, taking a dream vacation, owning a fancy new home and enjoying the good life while our country is crumbling down around you. Before you know it you won't have any life. I'm nothing but a crippled old man that has a young heart and an undying love for my country and to save it from the thieves that are doing everything to destroy our way of life and our heritage. One of the big reasons that it's happening is because of illegal immigrants pouring into our country unchecked. If I was only a young man and with God given strength I'd lead a crusade against the evil forces that are tearing our country apart.

Now we have a so-called DACA program regarding the 800,000 kids and teenagers that were brought into our country illegally by their parents. The democrats want all of them to stay and be given citizenship. During any protest you'll usually find some Mexican carrying a sign about not breaking up the family. I agree with them about breaking up the family so when an illegal alien is picked up I'd deport their kids too. That way I couldn't be accused of breaking up the family and everyone should be happy. By law the kids have no right to be in the united states. The nit wit Obama created the DACA program even though he stated that he had no constitutional right to do it. Time has proven over and over that he was totally incompetent. He hired other people of his ilk and everything went straight downhill. Eric Holder and Loretta Lynch fit into his mold of thinking and just about destroyed the rule of law. Our country is over run by hateful and loud mouth people like Flo Rectum who seems to have a bad case of shooting her mouth off and has no idea what she's talking about. Just someone else that can't get over Hillary losing the race. Looking at her and watching her behavior I think I know what she needs but I won't get into that for now.

The Emmy awards show of 2017 was a complete directory of every moron in Hollywood. It was nothing but a show to bash President Trump and I was really disappointed to see Dolly Parton on stage standing between two of Hollywood's biggest assholes as they bashed President Trump and she didn't say one word of objection. I'm sorry Dolly, but you caved in when you should have defended the President. If you were aware of what they were going to do you should never had appeared on stage with them. You had a good opportunity to show that crowd of liberals that you had grit and respected the President. All the jerks in the audience are there basically for one reason, to out shine everyone else. For me, it only represented a large crowd of ass-holes and nothing else. Of course the number one asshole in America was there looking older then father time, Robert Deniro. He's washed up as an actor but maybe since he's so liberal some producer will give him a part to play. I kept looking for my favorite actress, Linda Lovelace, but she never showed up. She should have won an Oscar in the movie deep throat and probably has more talent then anyone of the other females in the building. I've learned that being pretty doesn't necessarily mean that you're intelligent. On the other hand look at Flo Rectum, on the television show the view. Can being old and ugly make a person stupid? Rachael Madcow, another Trump hater who has a television show that has been guilty of reporting fake news is one tough looking gal. It's a shame that she doesn't join the Republican Party and help President Trump to drain the swamp. Then there's one that scares me when I look at her. She always seems to dress for Halloween wearing extra large colorful cowboy hats and huge dark sunglasses. Being scary looking and on the ugly side she now thinks that she's a rock star. I understand that her name is Frederica Wilson and she's actually a Florida representative.

I've publicized numerous times that my confidence in the human race is in the toilet. Serving 25 years in law enforcement and seeing how a once proud department slowly evolved into a kiss ass department shook my timbers. The department was taken over by supervisors represented by the politically correct concept and if you wanted to aspire and move up it was a requirement to kiss someone's ass. Even promotional exams were dropped and the department created what they called an assessment center so they could promote whoever they pleased and experience, knowledge and education had nothing to do with it. The entire attitude of running a police department and enforcing the law on the streets was effected until it became necessary for an officer to kiss everyone's ass in order to get anything done. I began to realize that I was a dinosaur and would never fit in so I chose retirement. It didn't surprise me then or even now to hear that someone got their ass kicked by an officer on the roadside. It seemed like it was becoming the only way any justice was to be realized. I've seen thieves of every kind walk out of courtrooms free as a bird with no adjudication of guilt and back on the streets to do it again. Too many criminal trials result in nothing more then a miscarriage of justice. Like I've said before the only justice that some scumbag will receive is on the roadside. I had to retire because I got too old to kick someone's ass and I just couldn't stomach having to start kissing ass. I looked all through the job description of being a police officer and never found anything saying that I had to kiss someone's ass in the performance of my duty. Too many police chiefs, mayors and managers subscribe to the idea of ass kissing instead of ass kicking and demoralized the police from being effective and doing their job. Rest assured the concept of roadside justice was born out of necessity. You can call it police brutality or anything else you want to label it but I call it roadside justice. When some punk assaulted me I tried my level best to unscrew his brainless head and you're welcome to call it anything you please. I strongly suggest that if someone objects to the officer's behavior, then stop bitching about it, join the department and get your ass kicked a few times. After your ass gets kicked good let's see if it effects your anti police attitude.

It appears that Washington, D.C. and members of congress are nothing more then a sewer. In my opinion just about all of the sorry bastards are nothing more then self serving thieves. Of course why would you expect otherwise, almost all of them are lawyers. I hired a lawyer that I will call Eddie blabbermouth and the only thing he was good at was throwing me underneath the bus and then lying about it. I appeared before judges that wouldn't recognize the truth if it hit them in the face. The judges and lawyers know who I'm talking about and all of them can kiss my ass on their way to hell. Everyone should do themselves a favor, read "Kangaroo Justice" so they can see how easily lying lawyers and incompetent judges can destroy your life and it's perfectly legal according to them. In reality lawyers have a license to steal issued to them from some law school they routinely rob people and don't even have to have a gun or wear a mask. They wear a nice suit, carry a briefcase in place of a gun and with the help of a judge strip you clean of everything you have. No doubt that judge in Ohio made a bad and unfair decision against some client just like the one that was made against me in North Carolina.

Regarding the Democratic Party, I have to laugh my ass off seeing how they insisted on the Russian connection with President Trump and how it has come around to bite them on the ass. After a year of investigations by a special counselor there is absolutely no evidence of collusion between the Russians and the Trump campaign. It appears that the investigation headed by Mueller, who was a former director of the FBI has selected too many Trump haters to the investigation effort. It appears that President Trump or anyone else is playing against a stacked deck. If they ever get around to investigating crooked Hillary she'll get indicted for everything short of the Lincoln assassination because she's had her finger into everything. I have to laugh when they refer to Hillary as the first lady. First lady my ass, the first lady was underneath the desk in the oval office giving Bill a blowjob. That officially made Hillary the second lady. Everyone should remember getting a blowjob is not having sex according to Bill Clinton. Have all the married men tell that to their wives and see if they buy it.

It appears that we're living in a time and age where everyone wants something for nothing. For example, look how the ladies are coming out of the woodwork claiming that so and so touched their ass forty years ago and they want to be compensated. Maybe they're just frustrated because they have gotten so old that no one wants to touch their ass anymore. Every time I turn around some woman is accusing some politician or movie actor of groping their ass. This ass grabbing has gotten completely out of control and men are being destroyed career-wise and probably family wise with nothing more then an accusation. What ever happened to innocent until proven guilty? These women should have to prove their case and men should not be denied due process. When I was growing up I use to always open a door for a female but now she might say that I was opening my fly to show her that little soldier standing at attention where in reality it would show a little soldier asleep on two sand bags. Men had better wake up because their lust and desire for that little thing that a woman has will destroy them. It's amazing that such a little thing can cause men to lie, steal, cheat and kill for it. I've known very few adultery free marriages . A marriage license isn't worth the paper it's written on when the juices start running for the excitement of an affair.

I have a pet cat that I love and respect more than 90% of the human beings I know. I've just about lost all my confidence in the human race. It seems to be part of their makeup to lie, steal, cheat and kill each other. One day they're happy lovers and six months later they're busy as hell cheating on each other. To me the marriage institution has died a slow death. I believe that men and women are far better off just living together and not getting legally entangled.

One thing that comes to my mind about the police department that I was on. When I went up for the rank of captain I had about as much chance of being promoted as a snowball in hell. On the interview panel was a black female that seem to be more interested in who I slept with then my supervisory abilities. I was a white southerner with the name of Robert E. Lee. She asked me if I had ever been intimate with someone of a different culture. I knew exactly where the bitch was coming from and told her not to worry because some of my best friends were black. I realized that I was doomed as far as being promoted because she had already labeled me as a racist. If there was a racist in the room it was her and she should never have been on the panel. During those times it was rough being white because the department was only interested in filling upper management positions with blacks.

When they stopped the draft it was the nail in the coffin of self respect. The greatest generation certainly belongs to the 7,000 brave young men who lost their lives on Iwo Jima fighting for the freedom that the present spineless generation of today is enjoying. It was the worse loss of life for the Marine Corps in any battle during world war two. I always remember those heroic brave men every time I hear of the NFL football players taking a knee disrespecting our flag, the national anthem and those poor dead young men on Iwo Jima. You sorry assholes make my blood boil and to hell with all of you. Running up and down a football field sure as hell doesn't define courage in the least. Running onto a beach head in front of incoming machine gun fire and then you'll know what defines courage. For me personally I wouldn't give the life of one of those brave young men for all of those ungrateful half wits in the NFL who disrespects our country. Enough said for those morons.

For all of you people that take confidence in the so-called "rule of law" and "due process" you had better wake up and smell the roses so to speak. The Fifth Amendment to the constitution states that no one can be deprived of life, liberty or property without the due process of law. I'm here to tell you that if you take that at face value then you're in for a real awakening. Nothing in that statement doesn't take into consideration that officers of the court known as lawyers will lie under oath to hell and back and will rob you of everything you have including your life if necessary. All of those fancy words means nothing to a lying lawyer and a careless judge. As in my personal case outlined in the book "Kangaroo Justice," you'll see how lawyers think absolutely nothing of lying under oath. The judges that I encountered couldn't care less if they lied until they turned blue in the face. Your Fifth Amendment rights were just about as equal as pissing into the wind. If you really want to see a miscarriage of justice and how easily it occurs, read Kangaroo Justice.

It's about how a trailer trash couple produced and distributed hundreds of slanderous posters with my wife's picture all over the county including the front door of our church house, to all our neighbors, on power poles, in the windows of stores, on car windshields and to passing pedestrians. I sued them for slander and libel and easily won a $35,000.00 judgment against them. They obtained a douche bag lawyer in Fort Lauderdale, Florida who was a habitual liar in every possible form. Between her and some dumb ass judge they turned the case around and made me pay them $125,000.00. It's an unbelievable true story on how my life was destroyed by the myth of due process. Between lying lawyers, senile judges and trailer trash people it has gotten me to the point that anything to do with the human race gripes my ass. For example President Trump gets three NBA basketball players out of a Chinese prison facing ten years for shoplifting and brings them back home to America. The father of one of them, Lavar Ball, doesn't even have the decency to thank President Trump for saving his son's ass. It was obvious to everyone that Mr. Ball was nothing more then a loud mouth ungrateful racist. After listening to him I could understand why his son was a thief. If his son had experienced a couple dishes of some roadside justice maybe he would have grew up to be a honest and respectful gentleman. On the second thought it would probably have been better if his ungrateful father had experienced a good case of roadside justice. Maybe it would have made him a better father instead of the ignorant moron that he is today.

Now we have a new trend working and the lawyers love it. All the lawyers have to do is get three or four women together and have them say that so and so felt of their ass and he will pay money to them even if it's a lie in an effort to save his career and marriage. Talk about a scam, this one really works. Do they have to prove that it happened, hell no. The accused is deprived of all his constitutional rights and the only thing he can do is pay up. I understand that Bill O'Reilly, who use to work at fox news paid millions to one lawyer that he had consensual sex with. He had to pay because it's my understanding that she made tapes of their meetings and saved all his incriminating e-mails. It was either pay up or she would bring their affair to light including his wife. He paid up big time trying to save his job and marriage but it all came out anyway. I'm no scholar in law but it certainly seems to smack on "black mail" and O'Reilly should have brought charges against her instead of paying her.

There's been a casting couch in Hollywood for years and everyone knew about it. It was just an accepted way of getting into the movies and no one objected to it.

I understand that good looking Rock Hudson had to suck on something beside a lollypop in order to get into the movies. It was during a time when everyone would do whatever was necessary to accomplish their goals. I just saw a video of Pamela Anderson attending a party at Hugh Heffner's house and she was walking around bare ass naked in front of everyone as she kissed on Hugh telling him that she loved him. Talk about trash.

When our forefathers drew up the Constitution I'm sure they didn't intend for elected senators and representatives to spend their entire lives in their political seat. Just for one example take Congressman John Conyers who is 88 years old and has been in office for 52 years. There are dozens more just like him and all of them need to step down and resign before they fall down from old age. It shows why we need term limits in a bad way. They will never leave office on their own because they love getting a high salary for not doing anything. If there was a lot more ass kicking on the roadside our country wouldn't have such a spineless generation running our country today. Thank God someone like Donald Trump came along in time to save us from ourselves. As much as he has accomplished in just one year we still have ignorant morons bashing him at every turn. Apparently the average run of democrats doesn't give a damn about what he has accomplished and they just blindly follow extreme liberals like Chuck Shumer and Nancy Greaserack. At present we have an overload of self serving assholes in congress that are busy as hell stuffing their own pockets and don't give a rat's ass about the welfare of citizens. Can you imagine the NFL paying the football commissioner Roger Goodell, millions of dollars for sitting on his worthless ass? No one including that jerk is worth that kind of money.

I recently saw some idiot on television sitting on a beautiful large alligator that he had killed for no other reason other then having his picture made. Hopefully by now that ignorant son of a bitch has been run over by a bus or something. The world doesn't need stupid bastards like him. He's a good example of why most human beings gripe my ass big time and why I love animals.

At present congress has paid out 17 million dollars to protect senators regarding complaints of sexual harassment from women and etc. All it takes is for some woman to claim that so and so groped her ass and right away congress pays her off to keep her quiet. Paying out 17 million dollars doesn't seem to bother the tax payers or anyone else which is beyond my understanding. Men's behavior will never change and neither will women when it comes to sex. As I've stated before men will lie, steal, cheat and even kill for that little furry thing that women have and women will continue using it as a weapon to get whatever they want in life. Three men that have been recently destroyed for the love of it are Charlie Rose of NBC, Matt Lauer and my hero Bill O'Reilly. Two more that got destroyed by a little thing that couldn't even bite you were Representative John Conyers and Senator Al Franken. No doubt there are dozens of well known people sweating it out right now wondering if some woman is going to hand them up too. If it's been so bad that President Clinton can get a blowjob from a 20 year old intern in the oval office then you must know how deep the practice must run in congress. Having a good looking 20 year old service you I can understand why everyone wanted to run for congress since it offered such a fringe benefit.

When Hillary discovered that she was playing second fiddle in their marriage she got nasty. She displayed a bitchy attitude toward the secret service agents and everyone else. Hillary was so busy wondering about that nice tasting cigar that bill was enjoying in the oval office that she ignored the problem in Benghazi and four Americans got murdered including our ambassador. They just recently captured and brought back to America one of the participants of the murder and charged him in a public criminal court giving him all the protection of the U.S. constitution. With that and a room full of lawyers they found him innocent of murder. It's a miracle that the lawyers didn't insist on awarding him a metal for his actions and erecting a statue of him in front of the courthouse. It's just another example of the service that lawyers provide. He should never have appeared in a public criminal court. His murdering ass should have been thrown into Gitmo and left there to rot.

Former governor of Arkansas Mike Huckabee, had it right when he said that calling Washington, D.C., a swamp was wrong because a swamp serves a good purpose and Washington D.C. is nothing but a sewer. The more I see of lawyers the more I'm convinced that being a lawyer should disqualify a person from holding public office. The entire atmosphere of ass kissing police departments and spineless politicians has completely disgusted me. During my career in law enforcement I've participated in a couple good size riots and have observed upper echelon supervisors standing around not knowing what to do and unable to make a simple decision. There should be no doubt in any rioter's mind that the police will use brute force in putting down a riot. Using a water cannon to spray water on rioters is a waste of time and water and serves no useful purpose to a mob hell bent on destroying property. If I was in charge there would be two options that I'd use with the water cannon. I would spray them with water containing a heavy red dye that they couldn't wash off for three or four days. That way the police could easily identify everyone that was involved in the riot and arrest their ass. The second option would be to spray them with raw sewage pumped out of residential septic tanks. When they are soaked down with urine and feces I don't think they'd continue rioting because they'd be too busy trying to get the hell away from the water cannon. They'd be more interested in getting their face and mouth cleaned.

Some people are simply born stupid as in the case of that washed up football player Colin Kapernick. The only way he could ever get any attention and notice was to become a real bonafide asshole. He was a sorry football player and would be better suited hanging on the back of a garbage truck picking up garbage and he'd have plenty to eat. He reminds me of a neighbor of mine who also has shit for brains. I have to laugh because they claim to be Christians and I can always see him and his hateful wife leave their house every Sunday morning all dressed up and going to church. It's a wonder the roof of the church house doesn't fall in when such hypocrites walk inside. Then they come back home and try every way possible to offend their neighbors. If people like them go to heaven then please leave me in the ground Lord. They sure as hell don't practice a Christian life style and probably can't even spell the word. I've seen my share of hypocrites but these two idiots have given a new meaning to the word. Hopefully I can outlive the trash and they will be buried face up with their mouth open because I intend to make their grave sites my personal latrine. This husband and wife team are bonafide assholes and seem to have complete control over the development that I live in. The development has covenants that are about as useless as tits on a bull hog. It's obvious that whoever created and laid out the development didn't know their ass from a hole in the ground. They must have been drunk on their ass or mainlining something because the property owners actually own part of the roadway easement. The association has given people that don't even live in the development equal voting rights as to what a property owner that lives in the development can and can't do. Anyone living out of state can actually control the destiny of the development if they own any vacant property within the development. It's fundamentally unfair that my way of life can be controlled by people that don't live in the development and have no intention of ever living in the development. Under the present rules it's absolutely possible for someone living in another country can become the President of the association. Just one example of how worthless the association's covenants are is the one dealing with operating a business out of a property owner's house. The owner can build anything he pleases in his so-called garage as long as he trucks it off his property and sells it on the street. In order to enforce this particular covenant the property owner would have to be guilty of advertising his business. The property owner could rent a billboard downtown or place a neon sign on top of his workshop and there's not a damn thing the association can do about it because according to the executive committee that enforces the covenants it does not specifically state that he can't do it. That's the same rational that was used when a property owner was planting trees on the roadway easement. We have one member of the executive committee that is a proven liar and thinks she's a clone of Ma Barker. The covenants are totally worthless as they stand and should be done away with.

The more I deal with people the more I love animals. In just a short period of time America went from the greatest generation to a present spineless generation. Generally speaking I have never seen such ignorant and dumb ass people in my life time. For example we have a real jerk by the name of Joe Scarborough who has a television show on the brink of closing down because no one watches it. He has said numerous times that he thinks President Trump is mentally unfit to be President while his wife sits there nodding her head like a bobble-head. These two dipsticks are nothing but losers and they know it. Our country seems to be nothing but wall to wall assholes because they are the ones that we always hear from. Take the skier, Lindsley Vonn, for example. She says that she will ski for America but not for President Trump. Hopefully that stupid bitch will pull a Bono and smack a tree breaking her chicken shit neck. Then we have some dipstick woman by the name of Silverman that stated on national television that she gets a scared feeling every time she runs up the American flag. My advice to her is why the hell don't you move to another country if the American flag scares you so much? What can I really say, just another asshole. Then out of the closet comes another dipstick by the name of Chelsea Handler, making a fool of herself by criticizing former governor Mike Huckabee's daughter who is the White House's Press Secretary. If Handler is really that nasty I can only imagine how bad her body parts must smell.

Three more that can't face the fact that crooked Hillary lost the election. Sorry, get over it and find a life. Of course Hillary can't get over it herself and I suspect that sometime in the future she'll be served with a stack of indictments three feet high. That chant of "lock her up" will finally come true. Unfortunately it will probably never happen because the people reading the indictments will be lawyers and they will fight among themselves seeing everything different in meaning. Words have a different meaning to other people and I'll give you an example of how it happened to me. I was sitting in my favorite neighborhood bar enjoying a beer on a hot sunny day, watching television and making a meal on a bowl of nuts that the bar tender placed in front of me. After a few minutes a nice looking lady came in and sat down on the stool next to me. Trying to be polite and thoughtful I pushed the bowl over in front of her and simply asked her if she'd like to eat my nuts and that's how the fight got started. I was only trying to be thoughtful and she misread my intentions. From now on I'll keep my mouth shut and let her get her own nuts. This nice looking lady turned out to be a transsexual and gave me a good ass kicking. Rest assured I will never again ask anyone if they'd like to eat my nuts.

Regarding women being sexually harassed it has gotten totally out of hand. I have to agree with Newt Gingrich, when he stated that men's lives and careers are being destroyed by women making allegations of sexual harassment by men without any proof whatsoever. A person is suppose to be innocent until proven otherwise but that concept doesn't seem to apply when it comes to sexual harassment. If you want to destroy someone all you have to do is round up four or five women and have them say that so and so felt of their ass and he's dead meat. There are some women that have used their ass to get a certain promotion and if that fails they can always fall back on sexual harassment charges. That's a lot of bullshit and everyone is entitled to due process which doesn't seem to exist in a lot of cases. I guess it's a wonder that I was never a victim of women accusing me of sexually harassment because I've been a muff diver since I was fourteen years old and I must have been good at it because I never got any complaints. Am I supposed to be ashamed about it? Hell no, I wear it as a badge of honor and had a lot of repeat business.

Look at Posie O'Ronald and see how her big mouth has gotten her dumb ass knee deep into a pond of shit. She offered two senators,

Susan Collins and Jeff Flake, two million dollars apiece if they would vote no on the tax reform bill. Then among other things she tells Ben Shapiro to suck her dick. To offer a senator money to influence his vote is a federal offense punishable up to twelve million dollars in fines and imprisonment as much as 15 years under section 18, U.S. code sub section 201 entitled bribery of public officials.

I've seen my share of hypocrites but these two idiots have given new meaning to the word. If I can outlive the trash I only hope that they will be buried face up with their mouth open because I intend to make their grave sites my personal latrine. This husband and wife team are bonafide assholes and seem to have complete control over the development that I live in. The development has covenants that are about as worthless as tits on a bull hog. It's obvious that whoever laid out and created the development didn't know their ass from a hole in the ground. They must have been drunk on their ass or smoking some powerful shit because they let property owners actually own part of the roadway easement. I have never seen such ignorant and dumb ass planning in my entire life. Sometimes it seems like our country is wall to wall assholes. Here's three examples to prove my point. Skier Lindsley Vonn, that says she will ski for America but not for President Trump. Hopefully that stupid big mouth bitch will pull a Sonny Bono trick, smack a tree and break her chicken shit neck. Then we have some dipstick woman by the name of Silverman, stating on national television that every time she displays the American flag she gets a scary feeling. What can I say, just another asshole. That's not bad enough, now we have some dip shit by the name of Chelsea Handler, criticizing former governor Mike Huckabee's daughter who is the White House's Press Secretary. I wonder what rock they jerked her from out under? Being under a rock I can only imagine how bad her body parts must smell that's just three more that can't get over that crooked Hillary lost another presidential election. Of course it has devastated Hillary and she still doesn't believe it and I suspect before it's over she will be served with a stack of indictments. Hopefully that chant of "lock her up" will finally come true and her husband bill, can stop looking back over his shoulder to see whose watching. It probably won't happen soon because there's still too much corruption in the swamp.

It amazes me how easily people misinterpret the meaning of words. One simple little word can have totally opposite meanings to another person. For example I'll give you an incident that happened to me so you can better understand what I'm saying. One afternoon I was sitting in my neighborhood bar having a cool beer. The bartender placed a bowel full of nuts in front of me to enjoy while watching television. I was really enjoying the nuts when a few minutes later a nice looking lady walked in and sat down on the stool next to me. She ordered a drink and in my effort to be a gentleman and polite I pushed the bowl of nuts over to her and asked her if she'd like to eat my nuts and that's how the fight started. I was only trying to be a gentleman and she completely misunderstood my intentions. From now on you can rest assured I will keep my mouth shut and never ask anyone else if they'd like to eat my nuts. This nice looking lady turned out to be a transsexual and gave me one good ass kicking.

Regarding women making allegations of being sexually harassed it has gotten totally out of hand. I have to agree with Newt Gingrich, when he said that men's lives and careers are being destroyed by some allegation that a man felt of their ass or made some sexual comment to them. The female doesn't have to prove anything and the man is deemed guilty based solely on her claim of sexual harassment. A person is supposed to be innocent until proven guilty but that concept doesn't seem to exist when it comes to sexual harassment. If you want to destroy someone all you have to do is round up four or five women and have them say that so and so felt of their ass and he's dead meat. There are some unscrupulous women that will use their ass to obtain a particular job or position and if that fails they can always fall back on sexual harassment charges. Thank God that most women are honest and work hard for what they get. It's bullshit to condemn anyone without due process which doesn't seem to exist in many cases. It's a wonder I was never charged with some kind of sexual harassment or whatever because I've been a muff diver since I was fourteen years old. I discovered that older women always wanted to take me under their wing and take care of me. I was used for every purpose imaginable to my delight. I always kept my mouth shut and never let anyone know about the relationships that I enjoyed so much. Most young guys always run their mouth when they get involved with an older woman. I'm certainly not ashamed of what I did and I wore my actions as a badge of honor.

Talk about another spineless wonder look at Posie O'Ronald her big mouth has gotten her knee deep in a pond of shit. She offered two senators, Susan Collins and Jeff Flake, two million dollars apiece to vote no on the tax reform bill then she tells Ben Shapiro to suck her dick. To offer a senator money to influence his vote is punishable up to twelve million dollars in fines and imprisonment for as much as 15 years under section 18 of the U.S. code, subsection 201 entitled bribery of public officials. Ben Shapiro responded to Posie and told her that she was already a felon and don't be a homophobic sexual harasser too. Posie violated a federal law and advertised it on the internet. Like I've said before you just can't fix stupid. Maybe her vision has been obstructed somewhat by having her face covered with hair most of the time. Then again maybe she's played the role of a man for so long she actually thinks she has a real dick. She is just another example of the now generation. When she was on the television show "the view" she displayed an undying hatred for Donald Trump and when he became President it was too much for her to handle. She eventually got her fat and dumb ass kicked off The View. She is nothing but a washed up has been that no one wants to hire. Maybe she should go kiss Ellen DeGeneres' ass and see if she can get on her show because they have a lot in common.

Let's face it, women are sitting on a gold mine and some don't appreciate it. Regarding Posie O'Ronald, it would tickle my ass if she gets indicted for bribery. Knowing her and what she likes I think she'd really enjoy living in a woman's prison.

When I call our present generation a spineless generation I certainly don't include our military personnel. Our armed service personnel are the finest in the world and by far the bravest. I admire and respect all of our fighting men and women in all branches of service. In the general population we still have patriotic citizens but that doesn't mean that we don't have millions of citizens that I classify as spineless. When the government did away with the draft they created a spineless generation. Instead of young men loitering around, taking part in demonstrations and amounting to nothing, they should be in the military learning a trade. Of course I'm sure mommy and daddy including the ACLU would scream bloody murder to force their little babies into the military service.

It amazes me when I hear some bleeding heart liberal say that people are starving to death in the streets. I've been all over the place for the past 83 years and I have yet to see someone starving to death in America. Where the hell are they? Are they referring to that crowd of people at the local welfare office picking up a free telephone and more food stamps? The only people I know of going hungry are the poor working bastards that pay taxes so the other free loaders can sit on their ass and get free shit. There are fifty million people on food stamps that eat better then me, so don't tell me that people are starving on the streets. The spineless generation of today has no idea what it is to be hungry and poor. The poor working people have to live from hand to mouth in order to pay taxes and provide a living for those that won't work. Work would scare the hell out of a lot of people that's milking the system. They make out better by not working and milking welfare. Can you believe it, half the people in America don't pay a dime in taxes and you can rest assured they'll be the ones screaming the loudest for more free shit. They have plenty of time to join in a riot and destroy property. Like I've said numerous times anyone picked up in a riot or property destroying demonstration should automatically lose all of their welfare benefits and have their worthless ass thrown into jail.

Regarding the question of poverty, I was born and raised in poverty and there was no such thing as welfare and food stamps. If you couldn't provide food for your family then everyone would go hungry. If it wasn't for rabbits, squirrels and polk salad we would have starved. Every time I heard Elvis Presley singing "Polk Salad Annie" I knew that he must have lived under the same circumstances as my family. Our old broken down farm house didn't have running water, electricity or plumbing and everyone had to gather around the fireplace in the winter time to stay warm. There was such thing as owning a car and if you went someplace it was either walking or hitching a ride on someone's horse and wagon if you were lucky. In order to get water my dad and older brother started digging a hole in the ground next to our house. They dug for weeks and finally hit water. They built a platform over the hole and fixed it so we could lower and raise a bucket for water. All of my brothers and sisters were born in the same old house without the assistance of a doctor. The only help my mother had during delivery was by a lady that was called a midwife. Luckily when I was born there was an old gentleman that lived closeby that people would call upon when an emergency arose because he had a little knowledge of medical procedures. When I was born it appeared that I was dead because my mom's umbilical cord had gotten around my neck and was choking me to death. The old man got a large pan of water and kept dunking me under the water until I started breathing.

I was born in the hills of northern Alabama and back in those days a person would probably live their entire life in one county without ever going anywhere else. A person could kill someone and flee to another state and he'd probably never get caught. In my home town the citizens built a large metal cage and if someone committed a crime or breach of the peace he would be held in the cage until the sheriff came to town which was usually once a week. No one in town was such a bad ass that the citizens couldn't get him into the holding cage. The town had wooden sidewalks and main street was gravel and dirt just like in the western movies that you see today. My uncle always carried his pistol in his pocket and one time that he was taking it out of his pocket it accidently fired striking him in the leg. Gangrene set in and he died from a simple wound because there was no medical facility in town or nearby to go to. The only person in town that could possibly help him was the old man that everyone called upon when an emergency arose. He always took on the role of being a doctor even though he never had any formal training. He did the best he could and everyone depended on him. Those were bad years and many died before their time. That was our way of life and I never knew that I was poor until my first grade teacher told me. Our school house had only one large room and it was divided up in sections from first grade to the sixth grade. During harvest time all the students were let out of school to assist in working in the fields. My mother and sisters always went to the cotton fields to pick cotton. My mother made a cotton sack for me because there was no one left at home to watch me. I would follow her as she picked cotton and she would always leave me some boils of cotton to pick. Many days I have seen my poor mother's finger bleed from picking cotton and she never complained. Years later after we moved to Miami so my parents could find a job I would go back to that little town of Beaverton and visit my aunt. I always worked when I was there and nothing would stress me out more than standing at the end of a ten acre corn field knowing that I had to hoe each row of corn. Now days you can't even get a child to mow the grass at home. Young people of today have no idea how easy they have it. Just thinking how hard my mother had it makes me realize what an angel she was. I would give anything if I could just hug her and tell her how much I love her. I will go to something else for the time being and come back to my family later.

I'll change the story and relate a more pleasant experience in my life as a grown man. I was having a cool beer in my favorite neighborhood bar when a big man walked in and ordered a Harvey Wall Banger. He drank it and announced in a loud voice that he had the best smeller on the planet. He said that he'd bet one hundred dollars against anyone to prove him wrong. Blindfold him and let him smell of anything and he would identify it. The bar tender challenged him and went outside coming back in with a box of wood chips. The bar maid blindfolded him and the bet was on. The bar tender held a chip of wood underneath his nose and he said that's birch. The bartender held another chip of wood underneath his nose and without any hesitation he said that's oak. The bar tender held another chip under his nose and he said correctly that's pine. The bar tender could see that he was going to lose the bet so in desperation he had the bar maid get on the counter and stick her ass up to his nose. After a few seconds he told the bar tender to turn it over and he had the bar maid turn over and stick her pussy up close to his nose. After a second or two he told the bar tender that he wasn't fooled and it was a shit house door off a tuna boat. To his surprise the gentleman lost the bet and the admiration of the bar maid. That bar scene reminds me of the time I went to the wits end bar in north Dade County to look for the scum bag thug that had stabbed my older brother a few nights before. I found the dirt bag and arrested him for aggravated assault. He didn't take too well being handcuffed and tried his best to get his buddies to interfere with the arrest. He kept running his big mouth and I decided right then that he was going to get his sorry ass kicked to instill a little respect in his attitude. As soon as I could get him into the squad car and away from the cheap ass bar I was going to see that he was going to receive some justice on the first vacant roadside I could find. It's the only thing that a dumb ass like him can understand. After I finished introducing the asshole to some justice I put his ass in a commercial dumpster and tore up the arrest form. As far as I was concerned he was nothing but garbage and the dumpster was were he belonged and I was satisfied that justice had been served. In those days a police officer demanded and got respect. In these days they get shot while sitting in their squad car doing paperwork. On duty one night I had three officers gunned down and killed so don't criticize me about roadside justice. That sorry son of a bitch killed the officers in cold blood and if I had the opportunity I would have enjoyed kicking his teeth out of his head. Don't draw up negative feelings about the conduct of an officer until you walk in his or her shoes.

I'm not a fan of Vladimir Putin of Russia but I do completely agree with a statement that he made. "not everyone is entitled to a trial." if someone is caught red handed at a crime scene then please tell me why the bastard is given a trial and a half dozen lawyers to defend him? He doesn't deserve a trial and I say stick it up his ass but good. In a place called Singapore, you don't dare spit gum on the sidewalk or do the slightest thing to offend the government or some other person. If you do it's your ass big time. In my twenty five years in law enforcement I've seen time and again where someone can commit murder and get away with it. If there's absolutely no question of his guilt justice would be served better if a bullet was placed directly between his eyes. It's either that or imprison the scum bag for 15 to 20 years at taxpayer's expense. I've seen crimes where the best punishment would be to have the scum drawn and quartered by horses. Simple and justified solution, take four horses, tie one leg to one horse, one leg to another horse and do the same thing with his arms. Then encourage the horses to run in opposite directions. That's what j call justice. Only when a person has to be proven of his guilt by a jury should he be incarcerated. When he is incarcerated for years he becomes institutionalized and you'd have to drag him out of the jail house because he wouldn't want to leave the good life. In jail he gets three meals a day, a law library, movies to watch, a basketball court to play on and female sex because the courts have ruled that it's cruel and unusual punishment to deprive a man from getting a piece of ass. Now maybe you can understand why they'd have to drag him out of the jail house. The whole thing is nothing but a lot of bullshit.

Sometimes people can't understand my style of writing because it's written so the common layman can understand what I'm saying without having to resort to a dictionary. What I say is unwashed and to the point and if someone disagrees with me so be it. When I write I also write for the mentally disturbed, ignorant, dumb ass and mentally handicapped which includes most lawyers and judges. I don't try to impress anyone with big fancy words out of a dictionary. A person's position in life doesn't impress me in the least. Just because someone lives in a big beautiful house, drives an expensive car and has a truck load of money they're no better than me or anyone else. When you're dead as hell you can't take any of your earthly riches with you. Always bear in mind that everything you have and own is only yours temporarily and that includes your nice expensive home, car and personal possessions.

During my lifetime I have seen the concept of justice slipping away due to the actions of self centered lawyers and judges. I've found that you can only get that amount of justice that you can buy. If a disaster occurs someplace within minutes the area will be crawling with lawyers like douche bag Mary of Fort Lauderdale, Florida. She still holds the record of being the biggest damn liar in Broward County. If you ever want to see what a lying bitch she is read the book "Kangaroo Justice" and you won't believe how easy a couple lying ass lawyers and two brain dead judges can destroy you. Someday that whore lawyer and her associates will have to stand before God almighty and explain what and why they

Destroyed my life. Hopefully they will be standing before God sooner than later that sorry lying bitch douche bag Mary, is a story in herself. I don't have a dirty mind but it sure as hell makes me wonder what she was giving to that lame brain judge in south Florida besides a sworn affidavit. There are three things that will always come out, the sun, the moon and the truth. Then she will be known for the lying bitch that she is. Her saving grace and the trailer trash she represents is the fact that I'm a cripple and limited to what I can do. I only regret that I never had the opportunity to give her a good ass kicking on the roadside. A good ass kicking might have given her some form of character because she sure as hell doesn't have any now.

A modern day Brutus, Steve Bannon, should have had his ass kicked a long time ago just for principles. I have to agree with President Trump, I also think he's lost his mind or smoking something besides Marlboro. As close as he's been with that looney tune book author Michael Wolff, I suspect that he's been responsible for most of the leaks coming out of the White House. One cardinal rule that President Trump should live by is keep your friends close but your enemies closer. Sloppy Steve has a big, loose mouth and apparently thinks too highly of himself.

Everyone needs a good laugh every now and then. The other day I happened to see Flo Rectum, who is still ugly as hell, screaming in a panic that President Trump is trying to kill all of us. She's had her head up her ass for so long she doesn't even know what day it is. I know what she needs and it's not more red dye for her hair. She's just one of many and our country is so saturated with politicians, lawyers and half witted liberal democrats that are completely blind to patriotism. They have tried everything they can think of in their attempt to bring down President Trump because they reek with stupidity. It's up to the strong to help the weak and stupid. That's the way the Lord would want it, so hold your nose and do your best to help them. They don't know any better and no one has ever recognized the depth of their ignorance. Unfortunately the only thing that will crack open their shelter of ignorance is a good old fashion roadside ass kicking that they should have gotten years ago.

They stand for nothing, they do nothing and their entire life is a big nothing. Half of the people pay no federal income taxes, fifty million are on food stamps and you can rest assured they are the ones doing all the bitching for more free shit. Our country is basically run by nit wits in congress. Many of them become multi-millionaires on their salary which stirs the imagination of an inquiring mind. World war two has been over for 75 years and we still have military bases all over the world that cost our country billions of dollars. There are 192 countries on the planet earth and we give foreign aid to a great deal of them that hate our guts and spends most of their time burning our flag.

Then we have nut jobs like Nancy Greaserack, trying her best to undermine President Trump's accomplishments by saying that all of the bonuses paid out to workers was nothing but crumbs. Really Greaserack? Tell us how you got so rich being a politician in congress? The crumbs are so pathetic? No Nancy, you're the thing that's so pathetic. Tell us about the private jet and the other properties that you own. Of course a thousand dollars is nothing to you and you probably spend that much eating dinner at some fancy restaurant some evening. I may add that the voters in San Francisco deserve you. I just saw Congressman Dick Durbin on television and he appeared beside himself. He stated that during the meeting he had with President Trump, the President referred to some country as a shithole and it was such a terrible thing to say. I personally have to agree with President Trump because there are a lot of countries on earth that calling them a shithole is giving them a big compliment. It surprises me about Dubin because he's been called an asshole for most of his political career and that never seemed to bother him. Asshole is a label that seems to apply to most democrats in and out of congress.

I have the perfect solution for the immigration problem in our country. If you're in our country illegally then get the hell out and that includes your kids too. Get in line like everyone else or maybe you think you're special or something. Guess what, you're not so get the hell moving.

Big business created the damn problem of illegal immigrants flowing into our country by the millions to provide cheap labor. Big business figured why pay an American worker $15.00 an hour when they can hire a Mexican for 3 or 4 dollars an hour. Every business hiring illegal immigrants should be fined $10,000.00 per worker and criminally charged. The Democratic Party is in complete disarray and support illegal immigration in the belief that they are going to vote democratic which just leads to more chaos for our country. Now of all things the Democratic Party in desperation is trying their best to get Oprah Winfrey to run for President. She has declined and said that being President isn't in her DNA but liberals won't accept her reason and still insist on her running. She made all of her money sitting on her ass interviewing people and doesn't know the first thing about running a government. Anyway Obama's presidency has just about ruined it for future blacks to run for office. Most any large city that is run and controlled by blacks and liberal white politicians are best described as shitholes or shithouses. I'm sorry to say but Oprah Winfrey would probably drag our country back to the stagnation of the past.

History will no doubt in time prove that Obama was an illegitimate President when his sealed college records at Columbia university are opened for the public to see. It is suspected that he entered the university as a foreign student.

I always laugh my ass off every time I see Maxine Pottymouth, the mother of all racist shooting off her dumb ass filthy mouth. Talk about ignorance she takes the cake hands down. Too bad she never got a good ass kicking on the roadside some place. It's like John Wayne said, life is tough and it's a lot tougher when you're stupid. I'm totally convinced that at least half the senators and representatives in congress would have made better men and women if they had experienced a good ass kicking every now and then. Getting your ass kicked good has a way of getting your mind straight.

During the meeting with President Trump at the White House regarding DACA, the border wall and immigration, Senator Dick Durbin, stated that President Trump referred to some nation as a shithole. If that's so? So what, who gives a rat's ass because it's a true statement. One thing for sure Senator Durbin turned out to be a real dick and his holier then thou attitude sucks big time. It just goes to prove the old saying, keep your friends close and your enemies closer. If President Trump knows that you're an asshole he'll tell you, so what's wrong with that?

Let's get on with the investigations of Hillary and the Clinton foundation so we can lock up her crooked ass where she belongs. She ran for office twice and lost both times, that should tell you something. I'll never forget how she'd walk out onto some stage, her mouth open, waving to the adoring crowd and grinning from ear to ear. She thought she was so loved and had the presidency in the bag. She wasn't worried because she knew that she couldn't lose with all the corruption support she had working on her behalf. You had a train load of baggage Hillary, and people could see through all of your bullshit. I only wish I could have been there when the election results hit her right between the eyes in total disbelief.

Sometimes I look back on my life and I wonder why the good Lord dealt my family such a hand of poverty? My mom and dad were good God fearing people and it seemed like we were in a deep pit of poverty that we couldn't dig ourselves out of. Even now as a grown man sometimes it seems so hopeless. My life has been destroyed by a lying bitch lawyer in south Florida and two brain dead judges that couldn't care less about what's right or wrong. They remind me of assholes like Robert Deniro and especially lame brain idiots like Sean Hasbeen, who will routinely kiss the ass of some dictator like Hugo Chevez. The jerk was recently in Venezuela telling the dictator that America was his enemy. I'm not a medical doctor but seeing Sean Hasbeen and seeing his love for a dictator starts to make me think that he has shit for brains. He sure as hell isn't a handsome person and appears that he's nothing but a washed up has been former movie actor that needs to get a life. Sorry, Mr. Hasbeen, but your best days are behind you and your future acting days don't look too bright.

Then we have Georgia representative John Lewis, who is a good case of why we need term limits in congress. He looks old as hell, haggard and worn out and needs to step down before he falls down. Doesn't it make you wonder how people in congress become multimillionaires on their salaries? As long as we have senile and flaming ass liberals in congress our country will never get straightened out. When people disrespect our flag and national anthem they need to have their ass kicked real good and don't feed me that line of bullshit about their rights. I'm sick and tired of hearing about everyone's civil rights. When it comes to our flag and national anthem they can stick their civil rights up their ass as far as I'm concerned. Our country would be better off if they had a foot in their ass. Where the hell was my rights when the judicial system was robbing me and destroying my life? If you think it can't happen to you then you had better think again. I've never met a judge yet that even gave a tinkers damn about what I had to say regarding my robbery and couldn't care less if a lawyer had committed blatant perjury or not. It certainly appears that judges and lawyers are perfectly comfortable with robbing some poor slob of everything he has and completely destroying him by an act of perjury. If you want to know how easily it can be done I strongly recommend that you read the book "Kangaroo Justice." The court will rob and destroy you under the guise of due process.. They'll rob you blind as hell and don't need a gun to do it. I respect the man on the streets collecting garbage more then I do of the lawyers and judges that I've had to deal with. When they die and go to hell they'll be busy as hell shaking hands with other sorry as lawyers and judges. If all of the sorry ass so-called officers of the court had their ass kicked real good on the roadside maybe it would have made them know the meaning of truth and justice.

It's like ole Benjamin Franklin once said, "We're all born ignorant but some work real hard to become stupid." Maxine Pottymouth, Posie O'Ronald and Nancy Greaserack are just three examples out of thousands that are more than qualified to be in the box of stupidity. Of course we have back stabbers like Brutus in the likes of Senator Jeff Flake of Arizona. His last name describes him perfectly and thank God that so-called republican is leaving office. He'd make a better used car salesman then a senator if he's even qualified for that position. I'm constantly hearing people in congress talking about what to do with the dreamers (DACA) and other illegal immigrants that have flooded our country. The democrats want all of them given citizenship so they will vote democratic and help win some elections for them. To me the perfect solution is if someone is in our country is here illegally then kick their ass out and I don't care if they're fifteen or fifty. In my opinion no one is entitled to a free pass into our country. I don't believe in breaking up the family unit so kick the illegal parents out too.

Every time I turn on the television set I'm subjected to having to watch some jerk like Joe Scarborough and his wife shooting off their mouth about something they know nothing about. I really laugh my ass off when I see and hear Senator Cory Booker of New Jersey say that he was really offended when President Trump used some vulgar language. President Trump was absolutely correct in describing certain area's of the earth's surface. It's common knowledge that black people often call other black people a nigger but don't dare use the term shithole. Cory Booker probably curses like a drunk sailor on a Saturday night and for him to say that President Trump offended him with such vulgar talk is nothing but a lot of political bullshit.

Former President Ronald Reagan described politicians perfectly when he said "Politicians and diapers need to be changed often and for the same reason." That certainly applies to talk show host like Joe Scarborough and his prop Mika Brzezinski, who will run her puppet mouth when Joe pulls the string. How does this hit you Joe? I believe that if anyone's image belongs on Mount Rushmore it's President Trump. He was elected and saved our country from total destruction in spite of liberal ass talk show hosts, the news media, the Obama administration and corrupt politicians, not to mention high echelon people in the FBI and department of justice. It's a shame that Obama didn't get his sorry ass kicked real good on the roadside because it might have had him grow some balls and appreciate America. He looked like a muslim, talked like a muslim, attended mosque to worship and thought that the muslims saved the planet and were the most intelligent people that existed on earth. My observation left me with the opinion that if it walks like a duck and quacks like a duck you can rest assured that it's a duck.

Between him and nit wits like Flo Rectum and Ana Navarro, they're proof of the pudding. They remind me of a couple good bowel movements. Navarro never fails to say that President Trump is guilty of misogyny. Please Ana, the people that attend or watch the program the view have no idea what the hell you're talking about. The view's audience and people of their ilk have no idea that the word misogyny means woman hater. Ana, if you want the audience to understand you when you talk you'll have to talk on a kindergarten level. You have to realize who you're talking to. Considering looks, Navarro would probably appeal to some drunk but I think Rectum is out of luck attracting anything because her looks would snag lightning. She's just one of those people that has worked real hard at being stupid.

Sometimes I feel like just giving up on the human race. Everyone seems to see everything differently. If two people see the same thing both will come up with different conclusions. Just to prove my point I attended a sporting event recently and the two gentlemen sitting in front of me kept arguing about what they see across the playing field. They were arguing about a nice young lady sitting on the bleachers facing them on the other side of the field. I overheard one gentleman say that he could see up the young woman's skirt and that she wasn't wearing any panties. The other gentleman told him that he was wrong and the woman was wearing panties. They argued about it until they offered a young kid sitting in front of them five dollars if he'd go underneath the bleachers on the other side of the field and see if the young woman was wearing any panties or not. The kid did as he was told and when he went underneath the bleachers he came out and shouted to the two gentlemen that both of them were wrong because it was flies. Something as simple as that and two people couldn't see the same thing.

Some day the sorry bastards that robbed me will have to stand good for it including the trailer trash now living in south Florida. These freeloaders have given new meaning to the term trailer trash and their lying cunt lawyer is no better. That sorry bitch thinks nothing of lying under oath and wears it as a badge of honor.

It's said that when a lawyer graduates out of a law school they take an oath that they will never misrepresent anything in a court of law. If you believe that line of bullshit I have some ocean front property in Arizona that I'd like to sell you. Any lawyer can rob people out of more money with a briefcase then Jesse James could with a gun. I came into this world with nothing and as result of the legal system, lying ass lawyers and brain dead judges I sure as hell won't have anything when I die. Whenever I see and hear a lawyer talk I suddenly get the urge to have a bowel movement. There's a thing of having too much of anything and that certainly goes for the law too. People say that we're a country of laws and that's for damn sure. We have laws coming out of our ears smothering us until it has created a situation where it effects our freedom and choice of life. Turn on the television and you'll always see a commercial about some law firm begging for clients. They have no scruples and will sue anyone for anything. Don't worry if it's true or not, that has nothing to do with it. The wall in their office is covered with law books regarding every law and no doubt if you fart in a restaurant you've violated some law and if a lawyer happened to be present you can expect a subpoena to appear in court. I'm sure it will involve the environmental protection agency.

Looking back on my life I only wish I had kicked more sorry ass then I did. Maybe I could have made a difference in the attitude of people toward our country. Sometimes I think that too many of the young people are under the belief that the government is suppose to give them everything while they sit on their ass doing nothing. The worse thing that could possibly happen to the young people was to stop the mandatory draft. At eighteen years old young men and women should have to go into a branch of the military so they can grow up and learn responsibility.

There are two kinds of people that I detest, liars and thieves. A thief will steal everything he can get his hands on including all of your personal possessions. A liar will destroy everything you hold sacred. Your family, your friends and your heart and soul. A liar can destroy your life and everything you stand for with little effort. I personally lived it when a lying lawyer known as douche bag Mary of a law firm in plantation, Florida took pride in committing perjury. Little did I know that this lying bitch wore perjury as a badge of honor. She had the ability to lead a circuit court judge around by his nose which stirs the imagination. Sometimes I think that the judge might be giving more importance to a blowjob then the rule of law. Everything that the douche bag wanted she got. It makes me wonder what else she got in his office. I would receive a subpoena to appear in court for a hearing ten days after the hearing was held. This made me realize that the judge was probably giving her something else besides court dates and she was really sucking it up, so to speak. That particular judge was another one that needed a good ass kicking in the worse of way to show him the error of his ways.

I've testified in different courts for twenty five years and far too often I've seen judges that didn't know their ass from a hole in the ground. There's a law against everything and if you don't believe it fart on a crowded elevator and see how long it takes for you to receive a subpoena to appear in court.

If you ever decide to buy a house be sure and check the neighborhood out good before you do. I didn't and I moved into a neighborhood that's wall to wall with pricks. Now I find myself surrounded by bonafide assholes. One thinks that he's the high sheriff of the entire development and tries to intimidate everyone. Calling him an asshole is a real compliment because it's obvious that he doesn't have both oars in the water and needs to be on a strong psychotic drug or in the hospital. He shows every sign of mental illness and needs help. I have another closeby neighbor that plastered his vehicles with Obama stickers and let it be known that he doesn't agree with and is offended by my political beliefs and planted twenty five huge trees between our properties to keep from seeing me. I thought he was a nice fellow even if his wife does run their household. Just because he doesn't have any balls doesn't mean that he's a bad fellow. In spite of everything I still think he's a good guy.

It's like ole Benjamin Franklin said, we're all born ignorant but some people work real hard to be stupid. Most of the young people that I've seen going to college are simply wasting their time. They need to be going to a vocational school learning a trade so they can go to work and move out of mommy and daddy's basement. Ask one of them about the structure of our federal government and you'll get a dumb look and a stupid grin because they have no idea what the hell you're talking about. Most are totally brain washed and don't have the ability to think for themselves. Unfortunately they are probably taught by so called college professors that hates everything America stands for including the President. I have a couple neighbors that loved girlie boy Obama and no doubt shit in their pants when I ran up my 4x6 Trump flag on my 35 ft. Flag pole. Neither of them know their ass from a hole in the ground when it comes to the south's struggle for independence known as the Civil War.

Washington D.C. has been proven to be nothing but a sewer and has been for the past thirty years. Things have a way of coming out overtime and that's just a fact of life. Like the old saying goes, shit happens. Recently one senator questioned Obama's manhood and if you think that the gay community doesn't extend into congress then you had better think again. The ones that you least suspect will turn out to be a pole hugger and couldn't care less about women. I watched that bowel movement, Nancy Greaserack, on television the other day as she was telling a story about her attending her grand son's birthday party. When the kid blew out the candles on his birthday cake she asked him what did he wish for and he stated that he wished that he could have brown skin and brown eyes like his friend. Greaserack, thought that it was such a beautiful wish and appeared to be close to tears. She thought that it was wonderful that her grand son wanted to be of another culture. It's a shame that anyone including that little boy can't be proud, happy and satisfied with their own culture. Instead of teaching him how to blow out birthday candles, teach him how to have pride in himself.

It's as plain as the nose on your face that the black caucus gang in congress represents nothing but racism and the undying support of organizations like the ACLU and black lives matter. Needless to say that the ACLU supports doing away with our national anthem among other communist leaning projects. Of course what can we expect, the ACLU is run by nothing but hair brain lawyers in bad need of a good ass kicking. Considering all the extreme movements in our country against traditions and heritage maybe the white Anglo Saxons should be placed on the list of endangered species. The way most cultures breed like flies it's obvious that the white race will slowly fade away into extinction. Our country seems to be wall to wall assholes and it's impossible to say who is the biggest because a new one pops up everyday. There are just too many of them to mention but anyone with any sense should be able to name and know them. Just for example the other day some nit wit so called college professor at northeastern college wished that President Trump was dead. It's quite obvious that he's one of those that worked real hard to become stupid. Like this nit wit some people think that growing hair on their face will make other people think that they're real intelligent. I could never understand why some people cultivate hair on their face that grows wild on my ass. Regardless of how much hair is on my ass it doesn't make me one bit smarter and that goes for a college professor too. The only thing that would make that nit wit any smarter is a good old fashion ass kicking.

I've never been in awe at another person's position in life. But that's another fairy tale that needs to be addressed at another time. After serving in law enforcement for twenty five years I've witnessed proud police departments go from an ass kicking department to an ass kissing police department which helped create an atmosphere of open season for killing police officers. Then we have a washed up douche bag like Bette Midler, shooting her big mouth off asking where is Senator Rand Paul's neighbor when we need him. She is referring to the idiot Rene Boucher, who assaulted Senator Paul as he was mowing his lawn. Midler and Boucher are just two more assholes that need a good roadside ass kicking. For myself I'm too old to have my ass kicked and I'm too young to die. Anyone thinking about doing it had better be bullet proof because I won't hesitate for one second to shoot someone's ass off.

I guess the best thing that describes my life at this point is a song that Eddy Arnold use to sing, "Make the world go away and take it off my shoulders." This time Lord, you've given me a mountain that I may never be able to climb. I never really appreciated being on top of the mountain until I found myself deep in the valley. It happened so fast and all it took was a lying bitch lawyer and two brain dead judges. I'll never understand why the so-called rule of law and justice system found it necessary to destroy due process. A lawyer like douche bag Mary thinks nothing of lying in court and having a pea brain judge not even question it. Of course this particular judge was apparently a good friend of hers. When I left the courtroom in North Carolina I had the distinct feeling that I had just been mugged and no street thug could have done a better job of it. I told the judge that he was wrong because he was dead wrong and it was a miscarriage of justice. Hopefully he had the intelligence to understand what the hell I was saying. As far as I was concerned he was incompetent and a fool. Someday that lying bitch lawyer will turn around and I'll be standing there. The sorry bitch needs to stand good for her actions.

It didn't help my day when I turned on the television and there was joy "bowel movement" Rectum running her ugly mouth off again bashing the Christian religion. The entire cast on the television show "the view" are nothing but a bunch of empty headed women doing nothing but bashing President Trump and the Republican Party. They really get nasty when it's that time of the month. None of them know what the hell they're talking about and when they're not talking they just sit there and look stupid. All of them need to get a life and stop exhibiting stupidity.

Always remember nothing is free. When you see someone on television telling you that they will send you a free bottle of whatever, it's nothing but a scam, so beware. As soon as they send you the so-called free bottle you'll be automatically signed up for their program and will start receiving more bottles each month and a bill for more bottles that you don't want.

I don't know what other people think but I'm convinced that most politicians are about as worthless as tits on a bull hog, especially those in congress. They're overpaid and should be paid for part time employment because half the time they aren't there and do nothing but sit on their ass. History has shown that some become multi millionaires by simply standing around arguing, scratching their ass and accomplishing nothing. Doesn't it make you wonder how people like Nancy "crumbs" Greaserack, has acquired millions of dollars in wealth and mansions just by sitting on her ass. The people of San Francisco deserve her. Most of her constituents probably live in tents, underneath bridges, in parks and any other place they can set up housekeeping.

Our country is presently faced with a crisis of school children being gunned down in their school house by mentally disturbed and sick individuals who go off the deep end. Rest assured, the politicians will stand around with their heads up their ass and do nothing but blame the national rifle association. Unfortunately most of the people young and old taking part in any demonstration regarding the incident that occurred at Stoneman Douglas High School in Parkland, Florida will also falsely accuse the NRA for causing the problem. They can't see the forest for the trees. I have tried tirelessly to offer a solution that will prohibit guns from falling into the hands of mentally ill people to no avail it's not an absolute position to take but it sure as hell will certainly suppress the problem somewhat. In conjunction with the background checks conducted by the FBI and local police agencies I feel that school shootings will almost be completely stopped. I certainly believe in the second amendment but I also know that any gun is an instrument made solely for killing something and great precaution should be taken in selling it to anyone. As far as I'm concerned anyone trying to buy a gun of any sort should be required to produce evidence that he is of sound mind and has no mental issues. If that had been law the children murdered at Douglas High School would be alive today. Of course no politician would ever support such a radical law because he or she knows that it would cost them votes and at present more value is placed on votes then a young person's life and the tail will continue wagging the dog. To me the lives of innocent young people mean more to me then the millions of gun nuts and politicians that object to there being a law. Politicians won't accomplish jack shit and the killings will continue.

Some things you can't completely stop and the best you can do is try to control and suppress it and that goes for all degrees of criminal activity. Seeing how human beings kill each other, steal from each other, cheat on each other and lie on each other has caused me to mostly lose what respect I had on the human race. I don't believe anything I read and only half what I hear. I've learned in my life to never confide in a friend because your friend today may well be your biggest enemy tomorrow. I have found that the best way of losing a friend is to loan him money. Never be in awe at someone because they might have a wall covered with college degrees. Believe me when I say that college degrees don't necessarily indicate that the person is smart as a whip and intelligent. Some of the dumbest bastards that I ever met were graduates of prestigious universities and couldn't hit their ass with a bow fiddle. On the other hand, some of the smartest people I have ever known were dirt poor, hard working and never even finished high school. I would feel a lot better if that class of people made up congress then what we have now.

When I was a young kid I would always hear my father saying that the Democratic Party was for the working man. That was when the unions were on the uprise and most of the people in the south were democrats. Well, times have changed and we now live in a different world and you may as well fart in the wind if you still think that the Democratic Party represents the working class. The Democratic Party and it's liberal policies almost destroyed our country under the rule of that empty suit known as Obama. No doubt former President jimmy carter, must be happy as hell because people can stop calling him the worse President that the country ever had. Everyone will know what a fraud Obama was when his sealed college records at Columbia University finally come out into the open for the world to see. That pot smoking girlie boy will finally be exposed for what he was. He kicked his campaign off to be President in the living room of America's best known home grown terrorist, Bill Ayers. This idiot spent most of his time burning the American flag and blowing up police stations. He is one of those people that needs his sorry ass kicked everyday and twice on Sunday. Of all things I understand that he is now a college professor at some dump college. Wouldn't you just love to be in that stupid bastard's classroom?"

I suppose that most people have had to deal with a legalized crook, better known as a lawyer on occasion. Lawyers are suppose to have a "code of silence" that prevents them from disclosing any information between the lawyer and client known as privileged communication. Don't believe that bullshit because two minutes after you walk out of his or her office they'll be on the telephone blabbing everything you said to their lawyer buddies. It goes back to their rule, I'll wash your back if you wash mine.

I could keep writing until hell froze over but before I close this book out I'd like to remind everyone that the U.S. Constitution was composed and written by old white men that placed their life and wealth in jeopardy for the sake of creating a country that proclaimed that all men were created equal in the sight of our Lord Jesus Christ. Hopefully the race haters and others that are bound and determined to destroy southern history will finally wake up and realize the truth.

Always bear in mind that northern slave traders worked with African tribal chiefs to chain and enslave their own people so the slave traders could bring them back to America and sell them to the southern plantation owners. Every slave ship flew the stars and stripes on it's mast. The Confederate flag was never displayed on one slave ship which most people seem to not know. Every slave brought to America was brought here by northern slave traders and the largest slave market was located in New York City. A news flash to the race hating bigots, the Confederate flag only represented a desire for southern independence. Contrary to popular belief the civil war was not fought over slavery but for independence from the northern states that were determined to suppress southern wealth and influence.

Before I forget, last but not least I'm southern, proud of it and I apologize to no one for my heritage.